To Steve

Happy Reading and I
hope you enjoy the pub
scenes! Kev.
18/5/92

A Ring of Rocks

A Ring of Rocks

Kevin Cully

Hutchinson

London Sydney Auckland Johannesburg

© Kevin Cully 1992

The right of Kevin Cully to be identified as Author of this work has been asserted by Kevin Cully in accordance with the Copyright, Designs and Patents Act, 1988

This edition first published in 1992 by Hutchinson

Random Century Group Ltd
20 Vauxhall Bridge Road, London SW1V 2SA

Random Century Australia (Pty) Ltd
20 Alfred Street, Milsons Point, Sydney, NSW 2061, Australia

Random Century New Zealand Ltd
PO Box 40-086, Glenfield, Auckland 10, New Zealand

Random Century South Africa (Pty) Ltd
PO Box 337, Bergvlei, 2012, South Africa

BRITISH LIBRARY CATALOGUING-IN-PUBLICATION DATA

Cully, Kevin
  A ring of rocks.
  I. Title
  823 [F]

  ISBN 0-09-175108-X

Set by Pure Tech Corporation, Pondicherry, India

Printed and bound in Great Britain by
Biddles Ltd, Guildford, Surrey

For
Tony, Peg and Celia

PROLOGUE

Dublin, late 1959. O'Connell Street in October. It is lunch-time on a cold wintery day. Ireland's broadest street is thronged with crowds of workers all going to, or coming back from, lunch.

Some head for the restaurant in the Metropole cinema. Others, less fussy, queue at the cafeteria in Cleary's store. Some are quite happy with a fry-up at the Pillar café.

It is a scene full of hats. Everyone, men and women, wears hats. Not colourful hats or hats worn rakishly. These are sensible hats worn jammed down on the head. They are black, brown and grey. The men all wear heavy overcoats of the same colours.

The traffic consists largely of bicycles. Hundreds of hats rise up and down with the effort of riding. There are cars too. They are nearly all black and most of them are quite old. If you took a photo your black and white picture would look like a scene from the 1940s.

In this most Catholic city many of the noontime crowd have either come up from the country or have relatives there. They have come seeking work in the capital of De Valera's Ireland.

A man emerges from a pub and crosses the street. He is a heavily built man, made more so by his thick, brown coat. Under his hat his hair is thinning. He wears a beard, cut neatly. He is almost as old as the century. His name is Jack Culhane and he is my father.

He stands at the window of Eason's bookshop and examines the display. After lunch he nearly always comes here before going back into his office. The window is full of attractive dustjackets with tempting titles. He walks up and down in

1

front of the window for a moment or two. His expression is wistful. Then he walks quickly away up the crowded street.

'Ah, feck it anyway!' Father said and crushed out his cigarette. At two minutes to five, he rose from his cluttered desk and turned the smouldering ashtray into the bin, wondering for a second whether he should tidy his desk. He picked up a file to do so but then thought better of it and instead let them drop on the pile of other documents he'd been ignoring for days.

Across the aisle Hennessy looked up and seemed about to ask him something but didn't. The little fellow just shrugged and went back to work. Through the grimy, tobacco-stained windows Father could just make out the darkness that was closing in. Hemming him in and trapping him in this place which he now loathed so much.

No! No! No! He shook his head. A person has far more to do with his day than to waste it here, day in day out. Of this he was now absolutely sure. More than sure, he was bloody positive. To stay a moment longer would be to betray himself. The pretence really could not be kept up. There would be a train at quarter past from Tara Street and he could make that easily.

Hennessy was back at work now. On the phone. Mrs Fitz was in with Sheridan. He could make out their hunched outlines through the glass of Sheridan's poky little office and smiled to himself at the thought of hanging on for possession of that. An airless cupboard and periodic visits from the neurotic Mrs Fitz.

Here and there phones jangled and typewriters clattered. As he let his gaze run around the room for the last time, he patted the collection of charcoal sketches in his pocket. Little scenes of Dublin. Nicely done, he thought. In his inside pocket he felt the comforting swell of his little notebook of thoughts and observations. They would show the way and guide him now, he was sure of that. He had worked on them for the past two years and he was sure they were good.

He crossed the floor, with its scrap of brownish coloured carpet, and, picking his coat and hat off the peg, put them on slowly and methodically, making quite sure that everything was comfortable. If he'd learned one thing in the Customs and Excise Department, it was never look suspicious.

He half expected a challenge but none came. Mister Morley, who normally never passed him without bringing up some problem, approached but then walked straight on without so much as a nod.

For a second he was disappointed but he banished the feeling. He looked around and was about to fold his newspaper into his coat pocket, but instead contented himself with a glance at the day's crossword before dropping the paper into the bin. It landed noisily but still no head turned towards him. It was almost dark outside now. The street lamps had come on half an hour ago. He turned the doorhandle. He expected it to jam and make a fierce sound but it swung open smoothly allowing him to step quietly out into the corridor.

He walked to the stairs and descended to the street. Behind him he heard the sound of doors closing. He sniffed the air and thought that it wasn't long to Christmas now. Funny how he always imagined that he could smell it in the air. Even as a boy he could. Perhaps especially as a boy. There were some dark evenings, crisp and cold ones that, combined with the smell of chimneys and fruit stalls, all gelled into Christmas.

He stood for a moment and relished the feeling. He quivered just as he had as a country boy all those years ago. At home, the big terrace house by the Bay would be cosy and glowing with coal fires. The children would be playing or doing homework and from the kitchen would drift the smell of frying bacon. He saw himself entering and being greeted with surprise and joy. The two little boys would rush him, expecting some piece of fruit and Mother would stand am-

4

azed. She might even be put out a bit at first but then she'd be delighted, he was sure.

He stood doing up the buttons of his coat and as he did so, he could imagine himself taking his place beside the fire, in the big armchair. He would stretch for his moth-eaten copy of *The Golden Bough*. The evening would be spent there roasting, with the radio crackling behind him until it was time for bed.

The next day he would rise at a leisurely hour and take up his position in the front room. The view of the Bay from the window was one he never tired of. From his walnut chest he would take his pencils and pens and ink and assemble them on the table before him. He had a head full of ideas that would develop nicely, given time. Time and the right surroundings.

From time to time friends would call on him. People he'd known for years, the valued ones, like Tom Whelan and Bill Moriarty. They would take their ease. *Lig na sciath*. There, in his front room, they would congratulate him on his bold move and the wisdom of his decision. Here he would be neither civil nor servant to anyone save those he chose to.

A scruffy little urchin approached with a fistful of *Herald*s. He put his hand in his pocket, smiled, and waved the boy off with threepence extra for his trouble. Then he turned his collar up and headed for the station. Crossing the Liffey, he felt the chill wind whistle past him on its way up to Kingsbridge. The river was choppy, slapping noisily against the quays. On the bridge, cyclists stood on their pedals and strained into the wind, their heavy overcoats flapping. Away to the west faint streaks of pink still shot between buildings.

It had been a beautiful October day and now the city was putting on a show of warmth and colour for him. Roast chestnuts! The smell of roast chestnuts! A friendly, wintery, natural smell, it seemed to augur well for him. He believed in portents. To him the shape of clouds and the way the sunlight struck them had a meaning. He couldn't always explain but only knew they had an odd way of affecting his mood.

The city seemed achingly lovely. Now that he was leaving it. He hurried his steps and hoped that there would be a moon rising like a new half crown over the Bay. The train journey would be lovely. Rolling along out to Seapoint. The quarter past would be just right. He wouldn't be bothered by any of the regulars asking him damn fool questions. Only teachers ever seemed to catch the quarter past.

He smiled at the young Guard on the corner and the young man nodded back at him. Fine body of men, he thought, smart fellas. They kept an appropriate level of order in the city. But for them, the gurriers would overrun the place. That was a part of the city, dark and menacing, that he wanted to leave behind.

He always headed down O'Connell Street from work and never cut through the mean streets that lay festering behind it. The foul language screeched by the women at their children in the street made him blanch. The bawls and bellows that came out of them would make a sinner blush to his roots.

He hated the stink, a sort of sour, bitter smell that came from the hallways and the cheap little hotels, and could hardly imagine how anyone could set foot in a place like that, let alone part with good money for the privilege.

Sometimes he would imagine himself in very different circumstances. Stumbling through these same streets, fallen on hard times. His job gone and his clothes in flithers. No family, no nice boarding house, nothing but the cheapest room in the dirtiest of these hotels. Just like the one he was passing now. There on the sixth floor, in a back room, he would die, huddled in a torn and dirty overcoat on a bed that was little more than a straw palliasse. Legion of Mary workers would find his swollen, rotten body and have it removed to a pauper's grave. He stopped and looked up at the building. Its Georgian elegance had long given up the struggle against peeling meanness. That could be just the place. He shivered happily at the thought and went on his way.

The platforms were empty, as he'd hoped, and he bought a ticket and made his way to the south-bound platform. The timing was good. There was a great boom of steam and the noise of pistons. Then the five-fifteen moved slowly down

6

the platform. He found a window seat that would face the sea. The train lurched into a false start, stopped, then moved off.

He sat back and thought about the momentous decision he had reached that day. His last day of work at the damn Customs and not one of those hounds would know a thing about it until Sheridan opened the letter he planned to send the following morning. A simple, dignified statement of resignation. No specific reasons given but spiritual marasmus strongly hinted at. None of the silly ballyhoo for him.

He tried to imagine their faces. Healy would miss him and he Healy to a degree, for the red-headed Mayoman was a decent skin fallen among shysters. Hennessy would be put out, as would one or two others, while Sheridan would merely shrug. They were the kind of boyos who would dare a person to do what he'd done but would never risk it themselves. Hennessy especially. The little man had a child's voice register whenever he tried to take the rise out of someone. His whinnying laugh was intensely irritating and he was the office creep into the bargain.

Van Gogh had never had money but he'd managed to get by. You just had to convince yourself that you'd set the right course. Van Gogh shot off down to Provence and had a great time of it. Never starved. His problems were all in his head.

The train picked up a few passengers at Lansdowne Road and then it was Sydney Parade and the sea. He sat forward in his seat to look. The sky was dark now and the moon was still low but it sent its silver light darting across the Bay like spears. Just as he'd hoped. Gunmen, gallants and ghosts, the moon was a ghostly galleon and all that. It made him happy just to sit there and think about it. A woman across the aisle gave his grinning face a curious look which stopped his mouthing and prompted him to look out of the window.

The train made its sedate progress along the line to Blackrock, where most of the passengers got off. He had an urge to get off with them and shoot up to Byrne's or O'Rourkes for a brace of pints. Then he could compose himself and walk home at his ease. He decided against it because it would take away from the surprise of coming home early. After all, tomorrow he could pop into any pub in Blackrock that the fancy took him. A boulevardier, that's what he'd be. He wouldn't wear this damn coat again either.

He sat back and continued to gaze, enraptured, at the twinkling lights of Howth until they disappeared behind the sea wall. As good as the Bay of Naples people said, who knew about these things. The Bay of bloody Naples itself. It crossed his mind that he really ought to consider it a priority to celebrate the beauty of the scene in print. It must be worth some tussle with the muse, he felt.

The train pulled into Seapoint and he could see the terrace with its streetlight. He rose and adjusted the window sash so he could lean out and open the door, then jumped from the carriage before the train had stopped, his momentum carrying him forward along the platform to the steps of the footbridge.

'Early closing?' Tommy, the porter, grinned as he took his ticket.

'Something like that,' he replied but he didn't stop to explain.

Tommy looked a little puzzled and he left the boy staring at him.

At the top of the footbridge he paused to soak up the sweep of the Bay. A passenger boat was leaving Dublin port and gliding out by Howth with every light ablaze. He wished he could hold it still and keep it there for nights like this. He sighed as he thought that now he could take as long as he liked trying to put these feelings into words.

Actually, he thought, O'Rourkes tomorrow. The last time he'd been in Byrne's the young bowsie of a barman had served him a pint of pure spillage. Bloody slops! A whopping great muddy pint of J. Arthur. The cheek of the boy! John in O'Rourkes was a very nice man who did his business and didn't keep interrupting you when you just wanted to sit and sip and be left on your tod.

He'd go down after tea. He might have to. There'd only be a few people early on and he preferred to be lost in a crowd.

A movement on the steps below him caught his attention. Miss ffrench no less. Miss two-little-bloody-effs-ffrench. Just the sort of person who'd quiz him uncomfortably.

'Evening Miss f-french,' Tommy stuttered affably in her ear and grabbed her elbow to help her up.

'Damn boy!' she muttered but Tommy took no notice.

She must be eighty if she's a day. He couldn't imagine what she was doing coming out from town at this hour. She was a frail little woman who wore a plastic hat pulled tightly over her head with the chin straps tied in a bow.

He moved away quickly. He didn't really want to have to help her all the way up to the terrace. She'd blather on at him about how there used to be a man on duty specifically to help the elderly up to the Avenue and into their carriages. Carriages! What would a family of withered Protestant schoolteachers know about carriages? They might have been there one time, but they were never waiting for the Misses ffrench, two small effs or not.

He glanced at the station office as he passed and he took pleasure from the high, blazing coal fire there. The room was bright and cheery and the big kettle was boiling on the fire. A smell of polish and wood floated out. Mr Keely looked up from his timetable and peered over his glasses at him. He sensed disapproval. The look said he'd no business being home at this hour when the rest of the world had a full day.

He went to the side gate, pushed it open and made his way through the dark up to the terrace. There was no one about and just a light showed through the frontroom curtains. The lawns were in a bit of a state too, he noticed, so there was a good excuse for including a little light exercise in his schedule. It could be a great inspiration to him to plough up and down on a sunny day. Hemingway liked to chop wood, so he would mow lawns.

He turned the key in the big wooden front door and went inside. In the hall he removed his coat and hung it on the black bog-oak stand. His wife peered up at him through the kitchen's steam. Her jaw moved to say something but nothing came out. He went down. His teenage daughters, Mary and Anne were at the table with the two youngest boys. They all looked amazed.

Later he would wonder how such a simple thing had

9

suddenly been so difficult to explain and would produce such a reaction.

He'd made a short, dignified speech in which he had drawn attention to the tedious and soul-destroying nature of his job. A job, he had gone on to say, that he had always detested for its association with petty-minded parsimony. He had made an eloquent case for the freedom of a man such as himself, to seek his destiny. Ends would meet, though, to be sure, there might be a little initial difficulty.

'Sure aren't the girls bursting to be out of school and working? A clever pair of handsome girls like them would love to be buzzing in and out of town. The city is full of offices all screaming for the right girls. And what have we here if not the right girls?'

He'd noticed the two 'right girls' redden and wondered if it was embarrassment at the praise he was heaping on them. He winked encouragingly at them, but they'd only looked away. He'd ploughed on.

Man must seize opportunities and create something from little. There was plenty in the pipeline to keep him busy and productive for months to come. Hadn't all his friends told him, time and again, how amusing and profound his stories were.

So, having considered his position carefully, there was really no alternative but to pursue his real interests. Anything less would be a betrayal and a tragedy. He had resigned his government position for Art.

All in all, it had been very well put and, despite his wife Ellen's gasps and exclamations, he had got through it without losing the train of it and rambling.

Frankly he was disappointed with the reception his speech had got. She slammed down a saucepan on a ring and shot its contents out on to the floor in a greenish wave. Then she'd berated him in language that he'd never dreamt she knew and which took no account of the children.

He was a dolt, a great lump and a waste of space, useful to neither man nor beast. Those were the kindest but there were plenty of others that he'd only ever heard before from the crowd at the Stadium's boxing nights.

'Do you know what it is but you're the most stupid, selfish man I've ever come across. You'd scald a saint with your eegit carrying on. You've not got one iota of feeling for myself or the children. How the hell do you expect me to pay the bills when they come in or have you given that a second's thought?'

He'd replied that they had savings. She'd screamed that they were for school fees and had flung a jug of milk on the floor smashing it. He looked down at the white mingling with the green. This hadn't gone as he'd planned at all.

'But the course I'm taking is not without precedent, you know.'

'I don't give a tinker's curse for your precedent. We're the ones who are important. Us! In the name of God, you stupid man! Don't you ever think beyond the next pint?'

'Gauguin. Gauguin for one. Now he gave it all up and went off to the Pacific. Didn't do him any harm.'

'Well perhaps you should consider doing the same for all the difference it would make around here. You don't listen to a word that's said.'

'But Gauguin made stacks of money as a painter in the long run. And his family managed in the meantime. They didn't starve. They weren't flung arse over tit out into the street.'

'That's all very well. But you're no bloody Gauguin you great gobdaw! You're a civil servant. A Custom's man for God's sake! And who said you can write? I'll tell you. Your saloon bar cronies I'm certain. And not one of that shower could sign their names after six o'clock. But you go and believe them, the maggots! Nothing but maggots the lot of them! They should give you a prize!'

The two youngest children had looked uncomfortable. They had shoved their food around and had begun to breath heavily and snivel. She glared at him.

'Go on out of it! You have them crying now. Get out and come back when they've finished.'

He hesitated in the doorway, determined not to be shown out like that.

'Out!' she screamed. 'Can't you let them finish without causing more upsets?'

He tried to reassure the children with a smile but it froze

11

on his face and stuck there. He had retreated quickly to the front room, slamming the door behind him just to emphasize that he was still a force to be reckoned with. They'd all think twice so they would before they trifled with him in his own kitchen. He huffed into an armchair and rattled the newspaper noisily until he found the right page.

2

Contempt! Absolute bloody contempt. That's all she'd shown. There wasn't any point in talking to a woman like that. Ah well bollacks to it anyway. What the hell did she know about the arts? A few piano lessons from a stone-deaf chancer in Killarney when she was a child. Chopin, she bloody wasn't.

He looked over the paper at the fire. A lump of peat fell into the hearth, showering sparks on his shoes. He stamped them out and replaced the peat. Can't even light the damn fire properly. Miserable smouldering thing! Wouldn't heat your toes, never mind this barn of a place.

Well, if that was the way things were going to be, then he'd just have to show her. Deep down he'd known this would happen. She was that kind of woman. Not a shred of imagination. Might just as well discuss Dante with the Balubas. It was his own stupid fault, really. Bloody silly to take a noble idea home and expose himself to ridicule. They weren't ready.

In his mind he saw Maurice Walsh strolling down the Avenue. Known by all as a writer. What a fine life he must lead! He could be like that. Living on his wits in the name of Art. No compromise and, if others suffered, then it would only be for a short time.

The great man favoured heavy overcoats and he always carried a silver-topped cane. Whenever he saw the writer, the man's step seemed light and free. He swung his cane with the air of a truly free man.

By heavens Walsh was never stuck for an idea. Every library in the country had a dozen of his novels on their shelves. Adventure of every kind poured from his pen.

13

If it was medieval Ireland you wanted then he'd serve it up as though the Statutes of Kilkenny had scarcely dried on the parchment. He could take you to Bloody Cromwell's Drogheda or Brian Boru's Tara. It was all the same to him. Madrid, Rome and Lisbon were described in minute detail and the fella had never set foot outside the country! That showed what could be done.

He rose from the armchair and went to the sideboard. From a shelf inside, he produced a walnut box. He took it over to the table and set it down. From his watch pocket he extracted a small, brass key and with this he opened the box and took out his notebook from his pocket. It was a little curled. That was from the train and he wouldn't be doing that again. He smoothed it and opened a page of careful writing. There was the proof. He could do it too.

Assembling all the other material on the table in front of him, he divided it up into piles that roughly approximated to chapters and subjects, and then stood back and surveyed it. He adjusted a few sheets into different piles. Not bad. Really quite an impressive amount of writing. Now was the time to consider trying to find a publisher. Maybe it should wait until he was finished. He wasn't sure.

Also from the box he took several fountain pens and a bottle of black ink as well as a sheaf of writing paper. These too he positioned carefully on the table. It looked very impressive, he felt. Now maybe she wouldn't take him as a total joke.

He knew what his book was about and how each chapter would link seamlessly with the next one. He'd been over the dialogue. Everything was ready. They'd be laughing on the other side of their faces in the office before much longer. He'd give Healy something to smile about over his lunchtime pint and the rest could go to hell. He looked at the writing paper on the table, crisp and white. A new decade was just around the corner. He would start in the morning after the kids had gone off to school. He decided that enough time had passed for them to have had their tea, so he went down to the kitchen. It all came back. Ellen bustled about with a great show of activity for no other reason, it seemed to him, than

14

to make him uncomfortable. If so then she was successful and he ducked behind the *Evening Herald.*

He had to whip it out of the way as she banged down a plate of flowery potatoes, peas and a chop. He tried to catch her eye and make a laugh of it but she ignored him preferring to stand by the little window and peer into the darkness across the yard at the Sheehans' kitchen.

He ate quickly, realizing that his sister-in-law, the resident aunt, would be in shortly. He didn't want to go into explanations or listen while they discussed him as though he weren't there.

As he ate the half-burnt chop he noticed the two boys were there. Liam, the eldest would still be at work and then probably not come home until all hours. The two youngest were playing with soldiers. They had their backs to him but he sensed that they wanted no part of him. It would be difficult to explain things to them.

He looked around for butter but could only find marge. He put some on the potatoes. She came and poured him tea, taking no care and slopping it into his saucer. He could accept all these things if she would only smile. Then they could get on with things.

Far away a baby cried and, as though on cue, the boys gathered up their soldiers and left the room. Something about the abruptness, the angry way they wrenched at the door handle, shocked him. He finished his tea and put the paper down.

For the next half hour he prowled the halls and stairs unsure what to do. He heard the front door open. The aunt was home. He ducked back into the front room. The home he'd planned as an artist's retreat already felt like a trap. He mustn't panic. He must not give way now. They'd come around in time. He would simply have to weather the storm.

He decided to forget the resignation ploy. Illness was the best course by far. The civil service was full of fellows who were off for years with little or no excuse. He would write in to Hennessy and enclose a note from Doctor Dodds. That would do the trick.

Feeling better now he took his coat and slipped out of the front door up the Avenue to Blackrock.

Sheehan passed down the other side of the road and shot him a sly, tipsy look. That old bastard wouldn't be long finding out. Farther along Mrs Winch greeted him heartily but he thought he'd seen her whisper something to Mrs Grimes.

Everyone knew. If they didn't they soon would. Lord Cloncurry hadn't this problem, he muttered, as he passed the dark squat manor house set back off the road. Different world. An artist knew where he stood with people like that. You'd get no joy out of the bowsies who lived there now. Not a penny between them. Fur coat and no knickers. It was beginning to rain and the moon had slipped into a fold in the clouds.

3

I was one of the children who sat, open-mouthed, during my father's speech that afternoon. I was one of the younger ones, the second youngest in fact, so maybe I got a little lost among all that fire and fury. That dark evening I chose the ostrich method and stuck my head into a plate of chips. For all that, the drama did lap over my dyke and I snivelled as children do when adults row.

When Mother said that we'd all have to pitch in, life seemed to go on exactly as before, the only difference being that now, every message run was an act of martyrdom, only done to bail you-know-who out. I quite liked that as it meant that I was at least on someone's side. Young boys like to be on someone's side. Right then Mother seemed pretty powerful to me.

On one such mission I left my mother peer-glaring across at the Sheehans as usual and I cowboyed my way up the Avenue. I took out the money and checked it. Ten Boston and a *Press*. One and ten pence. I hoped it was right. Things always seemed to be going up. Always up, never down. I hated that.

I'd hardly entered the shop before Edgar was looming over the counter snapping his pudgy fingers impatiently at me. When Jesus chased the merchants out of the temple, they must have looked like Edgar. I could see him in vast swathes of silk.

'Yes! Yes! What is it, boy?' He didn't wait for an answer but pounded off down the wooden slats that ran along the floor inside the counter to confront another customer. It was Mrs Gough from Alma Road. I was relieved to hear her being treated in the same curt way.

17

'Well really!' she said as Edgar lurched back and towered over me. His forehead gleamed with sweat and there was ash on his huge grey suit.

'*Press* and ten Boston,' I said.

'Don't you say please in your house?' he snarled.

'Please,' I added with what I hoped was a hiss.

'No bloody manners around here,' the shopkeeper barked. Then he whirled and snatched the cigarettes from the shelf and flicked them on to the counter as one might a playing card. He was quite agile for all his size.

I picked up the *Press*, with its damp print, and put my money down. Edgar swept it up with his paw and yanked open the till.

'That's not enough!' he yelled triumphantly. 'You're tuppence short. Are ye trying to cheat me or what?'

I'd known this would happen. Like I said, things were always going up.

'My mother'll drop it in to you later or I'll come myself.'

'Oh, will she now?' His tone was sneering and unpleasant. 'Will she now? That's very good of her, I'm sure.'

He glanced about the shop as if to say – look at this nasty, cheating boy. Trying to slip one past me.

I noticed Mrs Edgar standing in the shadows behind him. She looked flustered, as though about to say something, but she just sighed and retreated into the darkness. I heard the radio being turned up.

Edgar turned, distracted by the movement, and I fled out on to the pavement and down the Avenue. I heard him yell as I crashed through the back gate and sprinted up the path.

'You didn't give me enough money!' I raged in the kitchen. 'I was short and I hate that fella's guts and I'm not going in there again, I can tell you that!' Mother looked shocked. She opened her purse and counted some coins. Satisfied, she clicked it shut. 'Well the damn cheek of that man. I certainly did give you the right money. Come here now till I tell you but it's that creature who's the cheat. The ignorant fat puss. Hasn't the manners of a pig whenever he thinks there's bullying to be done.'

'I wasn't scared. He said tuppence short.'

18

Mother was unimpressed by Edgar's claims.

'Ah, that fella'd say the first figure that came into his head! I'll bet he's been below in Blackrock drinking. He can't add two and two after his session. I don't know how the poor woman puts up with it. My God but this country seems to float on a lake of porter!'

My Aunt came in and they weren't listening to me anymore but I was pleased they were making fun of Edgar.

'Protestant basket!' Father said, coming in and picking up on the conversation. He was glad to seize any chance to restore normality.

'Typical Protestant bigot that fella. Comes down here and thinks he can carry on with the same old Orange mularky as back home. Bloody Unionist! I'll tell him myself next time I go in there.' Mother sniffed at this threat in disbelief.

The sweaty Edgar had taken one of the Avenue's shops, which necessity made us use from time to time. People felt sorry for Mrs Edgar and it was widely agreed that she had a rotten time of it. Everyone had seen her husband coming down the Avenue, bouncing off the walls with drink.

Then there'd be shouts and bellows and more abuse for customers. He once threw a loaf at Mrs Kane when he'd heard her speak Irish, or so her son told me. She'd had to restrain her own husband from crossing the road and felling the ox with a blow.

Miss Ames had had a row over her dog. Edgar had lashed at it with a stick as soon as it nosed around the door. The dog had seized the stick in its iron jaws and yanked with such force that Edgar was sent tumbling over a tray of greens out into the street.

'Major's a dog who won't be bullied,' Miss Ames would say, patting the animal's grizzled snout proudly.

We had all laughed at that image, but on that day, when the laughter had died away, Father was left in the doorway, uncertain. He looked at Mother but she had gone back to studying the newspaper. Then he looked at me. I grimaced in sympathy and he shook his head and stepped back out of the kitchen door. I watched him walk slowly down the hall and into the front room.

'Oh there's a great man for the drama,' Mother said, turning a page. I wasn't sure what to make of it all. I could sense an atmosphere in the house but most of the time it didn't drip down to me or my brother. Mary and Anne only spoke of him in withering tones and even between Mother and my Aunt there were jokes in which Father seemed the butt. Liam acted as though he was completely unaware of anything unusual by being constantly going to or coming from important meetings in town.

When Father had first come home I had been afraid. Afraid that everything would be taken away. I saw bowler-hatted bailiffs at the door, flinging our poor bundles into the street, watched by sneering Edgar and laughing Sheehans.

Actually nothing happened. The civil service seemed to ignore his continued absence. We ate, went to school and still had our comics and toy soldiers. No one mentioned unemployment because that only happened to a different class of person. The class of person who didn't live on our Avenue. I always thought that that kind of person lived across the Bay in narrow streets behind the Pigeon House.

4

Dublin Bay runs from Dun Laoghaire all the way around the Howth. Well, it does as far as I'm concerned. I got this information from the adults on the terrace and they knew. Father was always certain of his bearings when he'd stand on the lawn and survey it. There were plenty of people down beyond Dun Laoghaire who claimed the Bay ran past them. This was merely jealousy, Father was fond of saying, because if you looked at a map then any fool could see that they had two perfectly adequate bays of their own, Scotsman's and Killiney.

Howth around to Dun Laoghaire harbour were the limits of the Bay we looked out on. Plenty of history too. This was a pedigree Bay. Vikings had slipped into this Bay. They were a wild and fierce group but they were glad to be out of the bad weather all the same. They'd stumbled ashore groggy and green-faced and founded Dublin because they had no choice but to build something to keep the rain off.

Thereafter Sistric and Ivar had a roof over their heads. Naturally the Normans, medieval hitchhikers, had found the Bay. They dropped anchor and insisted that only first sons should inherit property, much to the amusement of the native Irish who'd come down to observe their antics.

Much later Captain Bligh had charted it before departing on a much more famous voyage. All his efforts went to waste as far as the troopships *Prince of Wales* and *Rochdale* were concerned because they both went down with great loss of life because their captains hadn't bothered to consult Bligh's maps.

No doubt about it, our Bay and its coast were full of history. One of the first passenger railways ran from Dun Laoghaire

21

to the city. Just as well too because highwaymen on prancing horses plagued every road in and out of town. Terrible men and terrible deeds. Once giant rats had eaten a baby from a pram after its nurse had gone off into the bushes for a court with her young man.

As Dublin was such an important city, Westminster saw fit to dot the Bay with Martello towers to protect it from Napoleon.

'Boney was a warrior heh, eh, wha,

'Boney was a warrior, Jean François.'

But the Bay never did see Boney or his invasion fleet. I always thought that was a great shame because I loved to imagine the rough veterans of the Grand Armée marching on Dublin with their bearskin hats and huge moustaches and the British fleeing before them.

Edward VII, Fat Ted, landed at Dun Laoghaire to visit his loyal Irish subjects. They turned up in thousands waving favours. They admired his waistcoats but in truth they were growing out of monarchies and kings.

The city swelled and bulged in both directions along the coast. Its wealth and fame spread south and west into the country areas where people spoke of Dublin with a mixture of awe, fear and hostility but rarely affection. But they couldn't resist its power and they began to desert their smallholdings and make their way there, looking for work and an opportunity to make something of themselves. They looked at the pitiful, scrappy land and then, avoiding the eyes of their parents, they packed their belongings and went.

The settlement around the river-mouth grew and grew until the houses seemed to race along the coast and edge out the highwaymen and the baby-eating rats. These fled into myth and legend and were gradually only spoken about by scholars and my father, who made it his business to unearth such details.

The Bay showed all the moods and fickle changes that any stretch of water would and its shelter was no guarantee of safety for sailors or those in their care. You see despite Bligh and his exquisitely detailed maps, the Bay was cursed with sandbars that made navigation a nightmare.

22

Take the poor *Rochdale* and *Prince of Wales*. That was a fierce night. Their masts were shattered, they were hopelessly drifting so the captains ordered the firing of distress rockets. What was the point you might ask? These feeble squibs shot off into the sky at crazy angles while some did no more than hiss feebly into the churning sea.

Did anyone see their plight that night? There were only a few villas along the coast and their residents were safely abed, glad that the foul weather would keep robbers from their doors. The railway had yet to arrive and the tiny villages along the coast were blind to everything.

On board orders were screamed out, but ignored or snatched away by the jeering wind. The passengers screamed as they tumbled on deck and saw their danger. 'Oh God and Jesus save us!' they cried, while a nonconformist minister knelt on the deck of the *Rochdale* and begged forgiveness. But there was no God that night. Just red-faced soldiers and snarling sailors stumbling around hopelessly. Then a spark of hope.

'I can hear rocks and beach!' one shouted, and they all strained to hear. 'Yes! Yes! Those are waves breaking on shingle!' a merchant turned joyfully to the others. Sailors looked at one another and said nothing.

'Come on. Over the side. We can wade ashore soon. Just let us get a little closer.'

Joy and exultation surged through the poor fools. The sailors could hardly tell them of the jagged, razor-sharp outcrops of rock that the huge waves were now driving them on to.

There was no stopping the wretches and over the side they went like lemmings. I could hardly imagine what it must have looked like. My own Bay littered with their bodies for days afterwards. I wondered if any had drowned by Tommy Dorgan's baths where I used to swim in summer. I could almost imagine them lying among the rocks. Flashes of scarlet uniform bobbing in the shallows. Later the corpses would be black and bloated and eyeless, thanks to the meat-filled gulls that battened on them.

Along the beaches of Seapoint and Monkstown their bodies and belongings lay scattered for days. Clothes, provisions and weapons. I imagined barrels of rum and gunpowder floating on the low tide.

The city was thrown into uproar when the news spread. Rescuers went out along the coast road to offer what help they could to the few survivors who'd struggled through the surf. They were sheltered as best the locals could manage. There were no heroes that night, just blundering chaos and death.

Carraig Dubh. That's where we really lived as Seapoint didn't really deserve a separate identity. Carraig Dubh. Blackrock. There wasn't a black rock, not now in the modern times of De Valera, Devotame, our leader. There had been one but no one knew where it was or what it looked like. Not even Father knew but he had his suspicions.

There was once a swamp in the district and he figured that that was where the black rock must be. Once it had reared up out of the mire, like a horse, black as black could be. Easy to see why the first ragged-arsed fishermen called the place after it. They straggled in after a row with their cousins up the coast sometime in the fourteenth century, a pious monk noted.

There was no use trying to find out any more, Father said, because the country was missing half its damn history after the IRA had blown the hell out of the Custom House and the country's records back in 1921. Anyway the next thing was that the rock inconsiderately disappeared. Sank back down into the swamp which had thrown it up when Great Elk came down to the Dodder to drink.

Our home was a terrace of eight houses, substantial three-storey jobs, plus basement. They'd been flung up sometime in the 1850s by knowledgeable people who knew where to build. Each end house had a door of its own while the rest stood in pairs with shared steps. Three steps. Long and cool and made for sitting on in summer.

A coal hole was situated on the footpath and the coal went direct to the coalhouse in the basement. Down in this mysterious world, I was vaguely aware that these basements were sometimes separately owned. They were entered by a flight of steps from the terrace. Since the occupants didn't have

24

children of my age I concluded that they must be of a great age and were unable to move about much.

The road in front was badly in need of repair and was pitted with deep puddles that filled up with as much as six inches of water when it rained. It must have been so different back in the 1860s, I thought. Days of ambitious grandeur when people regarded the railway as a fabulous thing and its investors liked to live as close as possible to their shares. Easy to see and hear the rattle, creak and jingle of broughams drawing up and depositing men and women spendidly attired for dinner. West Brits all, full of drive and confidence. That Bay, with its wonderful view would always be there for them, just like their railway. They were lucky people to have such purpose.

Entrance to the terrace was gained through a splendid pillared gateway. At the top of each solid granite pillar there were wrought-iron lampstands. But no lamps ever burned in them and the gates that had once swung open to admit the elegant horse-drawn carriages, were now jammed open as was the side gate, used in those days by the scullions and maids who waited on the great ones.

The houses faced on to a strip of grass that ran the length of the terrace. There were two sets of steps down on to the lawns. There were no markings to separate one lawn from the next, for in the original plan all were equal and such a notion as a boundary or a hedge would have been considered impertinent in the extreme.

But in our times such niceties had vanished. Of course no one ever erected anything but they made absolutely sure that they knew exactly where their boundaires were. Some did this by mowing patterns different from the others, while others merely let their grass grow higher than their neighbours'. Yet another faction favoured growing flowers along the width of the lawn to match the width of their house. Others still, of the deepest rural extraction, used edging stones. We used edging stones.

It was vital for everyone to know where they stood on these matters. It was no longer a confident age. Atom bombs and Hungary had put paid to that. They had worked hard to get these houses and all that went with them. Some had made a long journey to live on these shores where they could see the pretty regattas in summer.

Impressive elms bordered the overgrown banks that sloped down to the railway line. Here was an area, out of sight, that the adults didn't dispute. It took care of itself. Dock and nettles grew in profusion with bluebells and snowdrops. There were sycamores and haws and evergreens rooting in every crack and crevice.

Paths and trails criss-crossed these few acres and each one was rich with memories of battles and ambushes, raids and counter-raids. The huge, sprawling Bug Bush housed our hide-outs and camps. I could see envious adults eyeing us as they passed in trains.

There was a bridge that crossed the railway line from our terrace to the sea. It had been built long ago by a railway company anxious for approval to afford residents access to the sea after they'd been cut off by the iron horse. The line to Dublin was straddled by many such bridges but our one was private.

We also had a little side entrance that allowed us direct access to the platform. The path down to the station needed constant attention and Father was often down there with shears, hacking away. More than one unwary resident had disappeared into the dense undergrowth on a dark, winter evening.

Across our bridge there was a circular formation of barnacle-encrusted boulders called the Ring of Rocks which we liked to think had once been a dinky little harbour from which young gentlemen in sailing boats made of rosewood and teak had sailed forth to picnic on the Bay.

How it must have looked in 1899 as the hampers were loaded and sailor-suited sons seated themselves noisily in the prow. Their fathers took the oars and with swift and expert strokes, rowed them out into the Bay. Wonderful to drop anchor there and fish all day, quaffing wine from cool jugs.

The remains of a changing room were clearly visible as were railings and steps, promenade and mooring rings. All the panoply of a confident little berthing spot. How my friends

26

and I wished that we could get out on to the sea. Boating would be the life but no one had such a thing as a boat on our terrace.

The houses on the terrace had been built with purely mercenary motives by people who would certainly not have been invited into them for tea. No, native gombeen men with a bit of ready cash and an eye for an investment had rushed to build them. Sites had been picked all along the railway and gangs of men had quickly levelled the land, laid the foundations and thrown up dream houses for the middle class.

The view seemed to attract people with grandiose schemes. Mother would tell of Major J. J. Kilfeather, who had occupied number eight for a period in the 1890s. People still remembered him on the Avenue, she'd say. A man of passion. There had been talk of how he had rushed off to France determined to challenge Emile Zola to a duel. 'That wretched Hebrew has insulted the Church and must pay!' he cried as he flung himself into a hack bound for the mailboat. Kilfeather knew no one in Paris and had not the faintest idea how to go about tracking down the famous writer.

As the weeks passed his rage dissipated itself in the cafés of Saint Michel. His money ran out and he had been forced to return to Dublin. His lack of French had not helped his cause and his only contact had appeared to have been an insane English Jesuit who had known as little about France as he had.

The Major had once been a wealthy man, so they said, but the Land Leaguers had run him out of Galway just like Boycott. He remained bitter that it hadn't been the word 'Kilfeathering' that had passed into the language.

'Knew Boycott. No good. Windy bugger!' he'd remark grumpily whenever he came across an item on land reform in the newspapers.

As the years slipped by poor Kilfeather launched scheme after hopeless scheme. None met with the slightest success. He sank money into a plan to run a hot-air balloon passenger service from Dublin to Belfast but nothing came of it. The world of business refused to open its doors to him. His sources were unreliable, his instinct self-destructive and his capital very definitely finite.

Slowly at first, but then with gathering speed, his creditors closed in. Strange men in tailcoats and battered stovepipe hats appeared on the terrace. They stood on the steps of the Major's house and battered on his door with thick blackthorn sticks. They were not afraid to make a fuss and a row. On the contrary, they glared menacingly at any neighbours foolish enough to venture to the door to find out what was going on.

They terrified the poor maid and barged past her more than once in pursuit of their quarry. The Major took to slipping out the back gate on to the Avenue but they saw through this and stationed a couple of roughs there. From then on, whenever he found himself bearded at home, he ensconced himself in the garden shed behind a pile of terracotta pots. Even the maid didn't know he was there and she could happily deny all knowledge of his whereabouts to the posse on the step.

Kilfeather began to appear shabby and unkempt as the noose tightened about him. He walked a great deal and rarely took cabs. At night he kept to the walls and shadows lest he be recognized. He went home after dark. The maid left with her wages in arrears and the house took on a shuttered and besieged aspect. If you stood outside at night, Mother said, it looked dark and deserted. But every once in a while, if you strained your eyes, you could just make out the flicker of the candle in the upper rooms. The Major flitted from room to room and paced about all night mumbling about Boycott and funicular railways. Then one day he wasn't there.

The door stood wide open. The creditors advanced cautiously, suddenly afraid that he might have laid a trap for them. But there was no Kilfeather. Their man had eluded them. Almost relieved, they began to help themselves to what little was left of value.

But Kilfeather had not really escaped. On his last, lonely night-time vigil he had decided what to do. He had got dressed in his best suit and had walked down the coast road to Dun Laoghaire. He had booked himself into a cheap hotel where he wasn't known. He had written a short note to his solicitor explaining that the jig was up and had then lain on the bed and had shot himself neatly in the head.

They found him in the morning and he was buried in Monkstown. He had no family, which people found most peculiar. They had decided that Kilfeather had probably done the dirty on them in the distant past. Mother said an anonymous donor had paid all the funeral bills though it wasn't much as it was a poor enough affair.

5

In those first few weeks following what he saw as his break for freedom, Father took great comfort in walking along the seafront. The huge expanse of the Bay with its familiar landmarks cheered him every time he strode out. The hill of Howth, Dun Laoghaire pier, the sand flats stretching away to Dublin and the Bailey Lighthouse all pleased and soothed him.

Crossing the bridge to walk along Brighton Vale, he noticed that there was a high, full tide. The powerful swell surged up and over even the big rocks, though it didn't succeed in dislodging the cormorants there. Down to his left Mr Keely was out patrolling the platform. From time to time Keely would stoop and remove an offending weed or discarded match from the flowerbeds. Even from the bridge he could see that the stationmaster's boots shone and on a dull day too.

He slipped down the alleyway and turned on to the Vale proper. Handsome houses and no mistake. Fine big windows and elegant columned doorways. There was no doubt that the British had had style. Beautiful dwellings for their fancy women. They were able to organize their affairs in the same way that they conquered countries, methodically and without guilt.

It was easy to imagine Castle officials sneaking out here on a Friday. They could hop on the train and forget all about the IRB or the GAA for the weekend and instead lose themselves in an orgy of silken stocking fondling. That was the accepted version of how the Vale had come to be and if it wasn't exactly accurate it didn't matter.

His eye ran out along the pier and then further to where a mass of white gulls could be seen gorging themselves on the daily movements of Dun Laoghaire's citizens. He would walk at least as far as the harbour proper and perhaps come back on the bus.

'How are you, Jack?' Moriarty tapped him on the shoulder. 'Wrestling with some particularly knotty problem in the great work?'

'Jasus, Bill, you put the heart across me, man! No, just thinking about the goings-on in these fine houses in the days gone by.'

Moriarty wore the heavy-lidded expression of a man with a cold. As if to confirm it he dabbed at his nose with a handkerchief.

'Then I wondered,' Jack went on, 'how much shite those birds get through in a week.'

'Ah, now you have me there, Jack. You have me there. I wouldn't eat one that's for sure.'

'And what is William Moriarty doing prowling the streets at an hour when all respectable people are hard at work earning a few bob may I ask?'

Moriarty's face broke into a broad smile. 'Oh I'm mitching for the day. I've a wojus cold so I'm going to slip down to the quare fella in Blackrock and collect a dose of something powerful to shift it. That's my excuse, what's yours? Shouldn't you be at home beating the jasus out of a blank page?'

'Strictly speaking now I suppose I should. However the muse has done a bunk on me so I'm airing myself for an hour or so.'

'That sounds like a pleasant sort of existence to me.' Moriarty stood back and looked him up and down.

'Oh, it's not all strolls, Bill, let me tell you. Far bloody from it! The thing is that I no longer work to the sort of time scale that you're accustomed to. It may well be that I'll get back home and face into eight straight hours of work. Right through to the early hours of tomorrow. You just can't tell. Every day is different.'

Just explaining his work methods to someone like Bill made Jack feel better. He would get right down to it when he got back he was sure of that.

'I must say it sounds great all the same, Jack. Tell us how is the work progressing. Are ye finished or what?'

'Hard to say, Bill, hard to say. It's going very well so far. There's problems, of course, but I should have a draft ready in a month or so.'

'That long?' Moriarty's voice gave no hint of criticism yet Jack felt stung.

'Well it doesn't just write itself you know. There are a million and one things that need checking all the time.'

Moriarty looked serious and concerned.

'And tell us now how's Ellen putting up with you?'

'Ah, she'll get better about it.'

'But you resigned, Jack, packed it all in. Quite a step.'

Jack thought about the medical certificate Dodds had supplied him with. Nervous exhaustion they'd decided on though Dodds had pointed out that it would need renewing and perhaps a subtle change of diagnosis to continue to convince.

'Oh yes, sure. Quite a step. But you know me. Never do anything by halves. Anyway she'll come round. As soon as the book starts to sell she'll be right as rain. I admit it's a bit hard on her at the moment.'

'Well, I don't know how you manage with the cost of things these days. You must have a nest egg or something. You Cork fellas are all cute. Listen here anyhow. I thought I might step in for a pint or three after I've finished. Would you care to join me?'

The idea was tempting. It would be nice to sit and sup and have a chance to chat with someone.

'Nice idea, Bill, but I really must get back to work. I'm only out for a breath of air. Honestly now, I must finish the bit I'm on. Once I'm clear of that then I might be round for a jar. Are you going to be there anyway?'

'Damn sure I am! It's not every day that I'm sick. I'm going to make bloody sure that I have a good time. So if you pass by, pop into Dolphins and I'll be in residence.'

He watched Bill walk away briskly towards the Avenue then continued his stroll until he came to the Martello tower. The great slabs of granite had a squat, reassuring look as though underneath they had long tangles of roots attaching them to

32

the ground. They would have taken some shifting back in the days of musket and shot.

He imagined the lives of the redcoat garrison as they spent day after day scouring the Bay for a sign of French invasion. None ever came and the great towers sank into disuse to open only during the summer months to sell ices and wafers to the crowds out from town to swim and play.

Or else they were rented by filthy writers like that fella Joyce. Great man now so they claimed but the book was full of filth for all that. The Yanks could say what they liked but Joyce wasn't capable of writing a sensible sentence in any of his big books and his shorter stuff was analysed by every yahoo with a BA looking for meanings that weren't there.

There were few people about, just distant figures wrapped up in their own business. He saw no one he knew. The nautical school caught his eye and for a moment he was distracted by the romance of it. A room full of young lads studying navigation and charts. Pity there would be little there to explore by the time they joined their first ship.

He descended the steep path on to what the winter had left of the promenade. He noted its battered and pock-marked appearance and treaded his way carefully along avoiding the potholes. Reaching the spot where the sand had mounted up the wall he jumped down on to the beach.

The soft sand felt good underfoot and the waves sloshed pleasingly among the rocks. He walked a little way down towards the water being careful not to get his shoes wet. The salt always left great white marks that were difficult to shift.

There was a jellyfish the size of a dustbin lid lying at the water's edge. Pink and purple veins radiated through it. He saw the brown poisonous trails underneath and was glad he had not encountered it while swimming. Still, jellyfish always meant a warm summer. So someone had told him.

His eye searched among the rocks, as it always did, in search of anything that might have been driven in on the tide. Today there was nothing and he turned to go. As he did so he noticed a flash of red among the seaweed ahead of him. He walked along the shore towards it. It appeared to be a red shirt, perhaps a bolt of red material washed overboard.

33

As he came level with it the sea sighed and pushed the object out from between two rocks. He rushed forward and used the crook of his walking stick to haul the body in. As he did so it flopped over and he saw the gull-pecked face of a young man.

The shock made him stumble back and sit down hard on a damp seaweed-covered rock. He stood up quickly and brushed distractedly at his coat. He turned and blundered away up the beach waving his arms feebly. He must have called out though he couldn't recall doing so afterwards. People stopped to look at him and point. Then, after what seemed like an age, they all began to come towards him from up and down the promenade.

Two fit-looking young men ran down to the edge and pulled the drowned wet corpse up on to the shingle. Jack sat on the edge of the promenade and accepted a cigarette from an older man. His hands didn't shake as he took it though inside he felt as though his heart was working itself loose from its moorings.

The Gardai appeared and an ambulance. A large – weren't they all? – Guard asked him a few simple questions to which he gave short lucid answers. The body was loaded into the ambulance and he was told he could go.

Later when he told Ellen and her sister, the man's slashed, blue features appeared quite vividly in his mind and he went very pale and began to shiver. Not even a glass of port helped so that night he went to bed early and lay awake for a very long time.

6

November stumbled along and the sourness spread through the house, clinging to everything like overboiled cabbage. Sympathy over his grim discovery had quickly evaporated. The dead man had not, in any case, been local. So Jack sat in the front room and picked over his coming home speech for the twentieth time. It had had a certain dignity, there was no doubt about that, but all his preparations hadn't taken into account Ellen's emotional response. She had not been meant to shout and scream at him. He never thought she'd do that. She had been supposed to come and link arms with him, supportively. Like when they used to go out in town. A squeeze, a brave little squeeze maybe. Instead she'd chosen to howl the damn house down.

He sucked air over his teeth as he recalled the horror on the faces of the boys. The way they had both rushed for the door, clawing at it like animals. Oh, their world had ended there and then. Shame had come home on the train to poison their lives forever.

He hadn't been invited to comfort them, instead they had run between Mother and their Aunt, asking again and again what would become of them. Ellen had bustled about clearing plates and making a great fuss over the fire. The coal had fallen out and her rage had been spent flinging it back into the scuttle by hand. Then she had riddled the ashes with a cold fury, snapping at the children and telling them that they would all have to help now.

Mary and Anne had reappeared and they had watched their mother spread her accounts in front of her. They had decided to be brave, like Ingrid Bergman, he had thought at the time.

They made a great play of going to work and saving the family. From his corner he had seen them scan the sits vac section of the *Independent* with an ill-concealed glee. Goodbye to Sister Aloysius. He'd hidden behind the *Evening Press*. The government was in trouble again but he could hardly take in what he read. He had half a mind to jack in the whole idea there and then and go back to the office. He managed to convince himself that he had a right to feel bitter and sad about the low esteem in which Ellen held him.

He saw less of the boys as the first month passed but the young were like that. They had no stomach for combat and had shrunk away from the adult war being waged over their heads. But often as he sat writing, he would glance up and just catch the door closing. Less often he would glimpse the startled face of the young crow backing away from him, to the safety of the hall.

Once as he stood in front of the huge gilt-framed mirror that rose like an organ from mantle to ceiling, he saw Mary behind him. He had seen her clearly and she'd been shaking her head in despair at him and her face had been pinched in disgust. He knew the girls loved their new jobs and he despaired at their efforts to make him feel guilty.

He began to visit the local library not just because it was important to have constant contact with books, but also because the action itself lent his day a purposeful air. At first he'd felt very vulnerable and had positively scuttled down to Blackrock. But he'd gained confidence and now he relished his outings and the comment he knew they provoked. Whenever he chanced upon people he felt were talking about him he would swoop down on them and take the steam out of their gossip with banter and jokes that really quite delighted them.

But it wasn't just a social event. He felt now that he was taking mental note of the things he saw and did. They would be useful. The way people talked and walked and held themselves were now important things to observe closely. If only they knew how he might immortalize them in his own good time!

In the meantime a project had begun to form. It took shape quite slowly at first and he wasn't even sure it was what he wanted to write. Then again its very lack of shape was an advantage.

He found himself devouring every book he could find on the great warrior chieftains of Gaelic Ireland. The librarian, tiny Miss MacEntee, was a great help and she happily allowed him to borrow more on his tickets than he was strictly allowed. She resorted for this purpose to an under-the-counter system which she reserved for favourites.

He wasn't sure how he'd become a favourite but he had. She even renewed his books without him asking. It turned out that she was an enthusiast for the period. She took a small pleasure in occasionally denting his confidence by some intimate remark about a book he'd never heard of.

So he read and took notes during that decisive November. Gradually the notes became speculation and then plot outlines. Characters took shape and form. In the front room, with its sweeping view of the Bay, there grew up impressive piles of paper which leant substance to his writing claims.

The boys crept back. On fogbound afternoons he would be startled by the wail of a foghorn, only to find them at his feet leafing through his books. Then he would sigh heavily and pretend to be annoyed. He would grumpily shuffle paper and move important tomes out of their reach and they would look up and ask him what he was doing.

He would draw a deep breath and tell them he was going to write a fabulous story set in the time of Ireland's last great heroes. An hour would pass as he told them of the Red Branch Knights and the Fianna and Cuchulann and Ferdia. Evil Maeve, the Western queen who sent men out to die for her greed.

While they listened, he could see the plains of Ireland, flat and endless, stretching away to a shimmering lake. The ground shook to the weight of the thundering hooves of the armoured cavalry of the Red Branch Knights as they flung back the Munstermen.

Well his book was going to be like that, he told them. Only better. His would be so much better. It would be a book of heroes, but a sad one. His heroes would be the last of the Gaelic chieftains. He would write such a book about their deeds against the invaders that they would rouse a patriot's blood to fury.

Then he would put on his serious face and gaze out at the white-shrouded Bay where mournful warnings underlined his solemnity. Then he'd shake himself from the mood before it took hold, gather up his notes, and read them over and over again with his pen poised for dagger-swift corrections.

Ellen never spoke of his work and only snorted whenever she had books or papers to move out of the way. He stopped taking his midday meals in the kitchen. The boys were in from school and noisy. She took to bringing him up a sandwich. It didn't mean a thaw. He found himself biting into half-cold leftovers more often than he cared for.

At the evening meal he would appear because he felt it was important for them to see him and he made sure that he wore a shirt and tie on these occasions. Ellen still washed his clothes and he was grateful for that.

Apart from dinner he began to stay more and more in the front room. He heard the boys tell their aunt that they'd been in 'Father's room'. He had recently bought himself a new sketchpad and he liked to amuse himself doing drawings of the Bay. He couldn't get it quite right and he found that the fault always lay in the shape of Howth Head, which never looked accurate no matter how often he did it.

He had everything he needed and his family seemed quite happy to carry on without him. The rift with Ellen would heal in time. With December almost on them, he noticed that he felt a genuine fear whenever he thought of the office. Nothing would make him set foot in that place ever again. Nevertheless he was glad that he hadn't actually resigned.

In mid-afternoon he would treat himself to a schooner of port. Port out of Oporto port, naturally. As he sipped it, he pondered the question of work. Sound men that they were, the Department continued to pay his salary but that couldn't go on. He'd had one surprisingly sympathetic note from Hennessy enquiring about his health but making no mention of a return to work.

He wondered how long it would be before they stopped paying him. A vision of court action presented itself but he pushed it away. No, they wouldn't risk that because the scandal would be terrible. He resolved to leave well enough alone. Perhaps they were paying off some kind of back pay or pension? He determined not to enquire. The kids' fees were paid and the girls were working. Liam could look after himself and the Aunt was an earner. A year and he could swing it. He went back to the shape of Howth Head.

7

There wasn't a single tree on our Avenue. Not one the whole
length of it from the top down to the pier. There were plenty
in the gardens but none on the Avenue itself. Successive
corporations had never bothered. Some felt that trees would
give the road the elegance it lacked. Besides our terrace of
mid-Victorian mansions, the Avenue was lined with the comfortable dwellings of the south Dublin middle class. There
were teachers aplenty, auctioneers and doctors too, but by far
the majority were those in the employment of the state.

Every morning the houses spilled out hundreds and hundreds of civil servants low and high, who thronged the station
platform and packed out the half a dozen trains that left for
the city far away.

There wasn't a department unrepresented there of a morning. Education, Transport, Public Works, Employment, all
turned up daily. Whole departments could have conducted
their day's work there on the platform and not bothered to
travel at all.

Then there were the semi-state. People who were something
or other in Gas, Electricity or Fuel. No matter how many of
them there were, none would have given up the journey into
the city. They all thoroughly enjoyed being part of the daily
bustle. They loved being jammed into the small carriages and
trying to read their papers with one hand grabbing anything
for balance. By the time the train reached Mr Keely's station
there wasn't a seat to be had. Often Mr Keely had to employ
hidden strength to squeeze them into the carriage and push
the doors closed behind them. They wouldn't have missed it
for anything.

The return was even better. There wasn't one of them who didn't feel a small surge of pleasure as they flung open the carriage doors and jumped on to the platform. The youthful ones would sprint ahead to be up and over the bridge first.

At the top they'd breath the clean sea air and say 'That's great news!' to one another and each knew what the other meant. Then it would be up the lane and home. Out on to their peaceful Avenue and their nice homes.

The houses they entered every evening were the sort that had had, until recently, a maid waiting to take hats and coats. But the young country girls had long gone off to England and the new ones became nurses.

Their presence lingered on in the attitude of many of the people walking briskly up from the evening train. The good old days were not so long gone that they couldn't hope for their return. Their houses still had maids' rooms, small airless boxes at the top of the house. Now children played in them but the owners knew what they had once been for and they sighed for grander times.

They treated the older residents with reverence because they were living proof of more gracious days. All that was left of it now was the hotel at Monkstown, set in its ways and its beautiful grounds above the Bay.

Through the iron railings could be seen immaculately trimmed walls, monkey puzzle trees over sixty feet high and rhododendrons so high they could have been small woods. Above it all could be seen the magnificent hotel. The architect, Mr Mulvaney, had been an admirer of the dream king's more fanciful castles. Commissioned to design a hotel he had sat up night after night poring over old books of design and he had included as many features as he could with the result that the hotel was a mass of turrets and towers, gargoyles and bowed windows. When it was finished it wouldn't have looked out of place in the Loire. The owner drew back from financial ruin and refused to include a waterfall, a gazebo of marble and a sixty-foot round tower. Mulvaney, miffed in the extreme, went back to designing stations.

The locals knew nothing of all this and were delighted with the penny-pinching building that they ended up with. It put a kind of full stop on the area. They had the Bay and the yachts and the railway so now they had the hotel to lend the district some sophistication. It became a cultural talisman for the locals. It employed proper uniformed staff and there was a real chef in the restaurant. During the yachting season and the Spring Show, the hotel was full to overflowing with English accents.

Locals who ventured there were suitably intimidated by the grandeur of the entrance, with its marble columns and huge staircase. It was exactly what they wanted. After all, they reasoned, a place where you felt too at home couldn't be all that special.

There were Nationalists in the area who damned the hotel as a watering hole for traitorous West Brits and their allies. They were fanatical followers of the tribal leader Devotame. For them, any praise for England or the English was an act of servility. Father, though a Devotame loyalist himself, dismissed the objectors as Gaelic fanatics and part of the price we had to pay for independence. Besides he felt they did a very reasonable afternoon tea.

8

In the months that followed Father's homecoming I joined my sisters and brother in a conspiracy of sulking. I say brother. Davey and I joined the sulk. Liam merely dug into his Teilhard de Chardin and ignored us all.

In fact I enjoyed the opportunity to sulk with an adult. In a peculiar sort of way it made me one too. Father was so obviously in the wrong and Mother was so enraged that it didn't take a moment to decide which side to be on. I sat with the others, wiped away my sniffles and looked outraged.

I remember his speech perfectly. He'd stood in the doorway of the kitchen and had told us why he'd left his civil service job. After he'd done Mother had exploded in a perfect foamer. I can recall the expression on his face. It was one of extreme hurt. He'd wilted before the onslaught. Trying to muster some small show of dignity, he'd drawn himself up and had left the room, closing the door quietly. Then he'd spoilt it all by slamming the door of the drawing room.

We were upset all right. But then children always are when grown-ups row. For days afterwards we crept around the house, fearing to draw the attention of either side. We were certain a catastrophe had taken place but we didn't really understand what it all meant. There was just a feeling that things could never be the same again.

Of course my father wasn't Jack Culhane to me the way he was to his office friends or to Mr Sheehan next door. Fathers and mothers guarded their first names in 1959. Adults were rather mysterious people who hid behind titles like Da and Ma. Jack Culhane was most definitely a Da. I found that parents tended to squirm when pressed for details of age,

43

Christian names and the like. I think they thought it might give us some sort of edge over them.

As the run-up to Christmas gathered momentum and Jack, Da, stayed at home and showed no signs of returning to work, we came to regard his presence in the house as quite normal. There was something comforting in finding this large, elderly, bearded man wading through piles of books. The atmosphere persisted. He and Mother weren't speaking. Mother's sister, our resident aunt, smoothed over the worst effects. This laughing Kerrywoman acted as an honest broker and stood as a bulwark of good humour between us and any ugliness. She succeeded by mesmerizing us with ceaseless jollity so that she became a parent herself.

Every day Father would come staggering up the garden path swaying under the weight of his books. He would huff past us and hurry to his front room. The great project was in hand. He would mumble things like, 'Just the information I need,' or 'I've been waiting for this fecking thing for a month! Great bit of stuff that MacEntee woman, really knows her chieftains.'

Historical. Something historical, I knew he was writing a historical book. I'd heard him mention Hugh O'Donnell. What I did notice was that every time he passed, Mother would immediately rummage in her basket and produce six or seven used cigarette packets. These she'd spread, opened out, on the table and slowly she'd tot up tiny columns of figures. These she'd hold at arm's length and scrutinize through her glasses. Father was to understand that she was doing the household budgeting.

Anne and Mary had the best of it. Not only were they able to take my mother's side but they were able to resent having been taken out of school and forced to work. The fact that they loathed their prim little convent school, and that working was exactly what they wanted to do, didn't matter. On the one hand they became part of the flood into town and could do exotic things such as have lunch in Arnotts or window-shop on Grafton Street before coming home each evening, and on the other, they were able to bitterly resent Father's forcing them to leave school early and forgo the chance of university.

They were being paid for sulking, which seemed a pretty good deal from where I was.

Despite the icy blasts from the loosely allied opposition, Father didn't seem too hurt. Sometimes he'd push his hat back on his head and look puzzled. He seemed then, like a man who'd accidentally blundered into a neighbour's house on New Year's day.

Being in his middle fifties he felt that time was against him. There was a desperation in his efforts to read the piles he borrowed from the library and each book held a dozen markers with scribbled notes.

My father had a past. Like a lot of young men who had been in the army, his adult life was blighted by the knowledge that all the adventure and excitement that the rest of us would spread out over a lifetime, had happened to him in a few short years. For my father it had happened even earlier than for most young men. At seventeen he had had the distinction of being the youngest Captain in the newly created Irish Free State Army.

The real reason for his early commission was that he could read, write and add figures whereas the rest of the volunteers were scarcely literate farm boys.

Seventeen. From that moment everything was downhill for him. What else could it have been? He'd driven an armoured train called the 'Sha' and had been shot at by Lewis-gun-wielding Republicans perched on every mountain top in Munster. After that everything else is bound to be a touch quiet.

I like history too so let me explain. Father fought in the Irish Civil War of 1922. That was that moment when, after seven hundred years of oppression, pillage, rape and murder by the heathen English, the Irish, in their moment of victory, decided to kick lumps out of each other.

Father had no real politics. He just thought that Michael Collins was a great leader. 'A fine figure of a man. The English were scared of him and no mistake,' he would say. He picked the winning side more by accident than by anything else. He could just as easily have belted his trenchcoat and joined the Irregulars.

45

My father's chronology was just the kind of adult puzzle that annoyed me. He claimed that he'd tried to join the British Army in the First War. I know they were taking them young but I made him only eleven. For all their exploitation of the Empire even the British would have baulked at sending an eleven-year-old to the trenches.

But the seventeen-year-old Captain existed all right. In a faded, sepia photograph there he is, standing outside a tent in his jodhpurs and Sam Browne. A close look and the years fall away and it's indisputably Jack Culhane.

For the most part his war consisted of house searches, endless patrols and the armoured train. Designed by an Englishman whose only word of Irish it was, the 'Sha' consisted of a normal goods train with sheets of steel bolted on to the outside. Nobody had told the great designer that the sheets needed to be set at an angle. Bullets whistled through it and Father had many trouser-browning moments in Kerry, where the locals tended to be on the other side.

If he fought for anything, then Father fought for order. Surprisingly for an artist he had an immense respect for the Law. Grandfather had been a Sergeant in the Royal Irish Constabulary. They weren't too popular at that time but fortunately my grandfather had retired to run a crossroads shop. In those far-off times the Republicans didn't kill men who'd retired and were considered out of the game. There was some dark muttering from his customers but he was immune to it.

He too had a small claim to fame as captain of the All-Ireland tug-of-war champions. Grunting sports like that suited a rural world of markets and fair days. He faded into history and had died by the time Jack Culhane settled in Dublin. All I ever knew of him was a handful of photos of a man with the luxurious sideburns and moustaches of the time, glaring out very sternly from among his team-mates.

In contrast to Father's accidental Free State-ism, Mother's background was impeccably Republican. Her father would have no truck with the Free State, cursing it as a betrayal. He'd been in Limerick jail in 1919, thrown there by the Black and Tans. After that he moved from town to town, selling whatever he could, hoping that the world would stand still long enough, just once, for him to land a punch and make his fortune.

He wasn't too keen on his daughter's intended. But he sensed that his own day had passed and he didn't make an issue of it. Jack Culhane seemed a big burly fellow who was going somewhere. Even if he was a Free Stater.

For weeks after the homecoming we crept into the front room on raids to spy on what Father was up to. He'd always be sitting mesmerized by the Bay. There were books, pens, rulers, rubbers, sharpeners and paper, covered in his neat writing. Being small, we played on the floor with our Dinkies. We conducted our guerrilla war at table leg level. I would lever myself up and peek. I could read the titles. They were all histories. Histories of Ireland's military past. The great and the glorious, warrior chiefs, the Battle of the Yellow Ford, the Flight of the Earls and the Battle of the Boyne. Glorious defeats.

There were other books by a historical novelist for whom he had little time. He felt that it was a simple case of luck that the man was in print at all. 'His stories are always obvious you know, and his characters are paper-thin. Oh, granted he does his research, but the things have no life! Now if I had the chance I'd write stories that would knock spots off them!'

He'd say that often as he sat by the fire and contemplated the covers of these books. Then he'd wrinkle his nose in disgust and cast it from him. I knew little of publishing but I imagined that a man with a beard like Father would have no difficulty.

We stopped worrying about him being at home. We didn't seem poor. We ate two or three times a day and we went to the same school. My sisters were working, but travelling into and out of the great city was exactly what they wanted to do. They now wore two-piece suits. Liam kept his business to himself and only appeared amongst us on Sundays. Then he would tell us how infinitely superior the Chinese land system was to our own while he munched steadily through a plate of roast pork. His flow would only be interrupted by our aunt dodging in to mound some more potatoes up in front of him. On those days I could see no change in our house.

9

Jack was aware of his heart racing as he stood and surveyed the piles of written paper spread on the table before him. His stomach clenched and he ground his teeth. He moved a few sheets from one pile to another. Not satisfied, he extracted a page. He read it carefully, but it meant nothing. He couldn't remember, no matter how he tried, where it fitted in. He picked up a pen and added a word or two at the end of the paragraph.

It's not working, he thought, just not coming together the way it should and that's the plain bastard fact of the matter. Jasus, I should never have thrown away those notes! First rule. Never throw away anything. You never know.

By December he had become aware of the enormity of the problem. It only emerged slowly. Not all at once. He could have coped with that. No, this problem had teased and tickled and deceived him. One day it was there, and the next day, not. But every time it came back it was a little stronger and more nagging. The more it reared up and took shape, the more he tried to push it to the back of his mind. He put down the sheet of paper and there it was, sneering at him. He couldn't write.

He nearly added the word 'simply' but there was nothing simple at all about the way he felt. Never, in his day dreams at the office, never, not once, had he ever doubted that he could write.

He sat down and looked out across the sea towards the city. They'd be sitting in Cleary's having a feed of lunch now, the whole lot of them. He supposed that his abrupt departure was no longer a topic for conversation. He found himself smiling at the thought of Hennessy's braying laugh.

Out by Howth a single white sail beat its way to harbour. It tipped over sharply as it rounded a buoy. He wondered what class of man had time for that at this hour of the day. There was a fresh wind blowing, sending swirls of cloud over Howth Head. Sometimes a flash of sun caught them. That kind of light made him feel sad, but in a pleasant way. He was acutely aware of his heroic loneliness at times like this.

He should have stayed away from the blasted library. That had been his downfall. Too many bloody books. Now, despite all his work and his notes, he was no nearer turning his idea into a novel than he had been at the time it first occurred to him in the office.

The closer he read his notes, the less sense they made. Names and dates were a jumble and the period, so long ago, refused to emerge clearly. The simple adventures of his young noble heroes had become buried under the weight of his own research. He didn't know where to begin.

This discovery of his own frailty made Father nervous. He didn't like to think too much about it. He'd returned all his books to the library and Miss MacEntee had looked upset. She'd tutted a great deal as she stamped them in. He had mumbled some excuse about other work and had fled to the pub.

He heard Ellen moving about the house. He wasn't going to admit anything to her and give her the chance to mock him. He glared at the ceiling. She was upstairs, hoovering. In his more thoughtful moments, he understood that she had a right to be angry. He must be careful and patient.

He began to draw little pictures on blank paper. Just sketches. He drew warriors in battle, dream castles and enchanted lakes. He coloured them in. It occurred to him to illustrate his book. Now that would be something. Imagine if he wrote a splendidly heroic story and did all the drawings himself. Not even Maurice Walsh did that. They were easy to do. They gave him pleasure and when he held them up and examined them, he felt that they were not without merit.

The next morning he went back to the library and borrowed books on illustration and drawing. Miss MacEntee studied his pile carefully as she stamped each one, but if she thought him

49

a hopeless gadfly, then she said nothing. Her expression made it plain that she considered drawing to be fit only to occupy noisy children on wet afternoons. He was not part of her special system any more.

A stream of designs and sketches rolled from his pad. Brand new colours, purchased in Blackrock, transformed them. He carefully labelled each one as it was completed and added it to his growing file. He knew exactly what each scene was and where it fitted with his story. He even had his hero looking the same from sketch to sketch and that was really drawing seriously.

He gathered up all his notes and, with great consideration, began to insert them at what he felt were suitable places.

'By God! There are chapters here!' he shouted as he realized what he was doing. 'I'm turning the damn thing into a book. I can see where it goes.' He was seized with an exultant glee. It seemed that every part of the story had been illustrated from beginning to end.

Father felt as though he had been reprieved. He was now back on course. A few days of pleasurable work had broken the logjam. It was wonderful and it was all he could do to stop himself shouting and rolling on the floor in triumph. He contented himself with a few low whoops and a quiet war dance around the sofa.

Far away he thought he heard a Hoover. A low humming sound, insistent. He would make Ellen proud of him yet. The bitterness would soon be a thing of the past when she saw what he really could do. Only the week before he'd made a joke in the kitchen and he was sure she'd smiled.

Now, as he read over what he had written before, he could see that it was rubbish. It made him blush to read such awkward sentences. The tea boy at the office could have made a better fist of it than he had. Thank God he had had the courage not to fly into a panic and make a total hames of it. He'd stuck it out. He felt good about that.

He took out a blank sheet of paper and wrote 'chapter one' at the top. Then he picked up his pen and began to write. Easily and fluently, the words came. One sentence glided into another and the sheet was soon filled. Then another one and another. At the end of the fourth sheet he sat back and stretched. His back was sore.

He stood up and walked up and down, holding his sides. Then he read it. It was good, no doubt in his mind. As good as anything Walsh had ever written. Just as good. Sitting down again, he fiddled with the pen. It was a bit difficult to take up where he'd left off. His mind was still buzzing with his breakthrough, he was on the road. There could be no more problems. The thing was all mapped out in his head.

That was it then, settled. He rose and strode out of the room. He could still hear the Hoover or whatever it was, coming from upstairs. He found a sandwich on a plate in the kitchen. It must be for him. How nice of her to think of him. He took it and ate it as he walked slowly up the road towards Blackrock and his pint.

10

On a dark winter night, Sheehan fumbled with his back-gate key and cursed as he dropped it. He stooped and groped around in the darkness and cursed as his hand came up with something sticky attached. He shook it away and gagged as a smell rose to his nostrils. Bloody dogs! As he fiddled to try and get his key in the lock he looked up the Avenue. He could just make out the dim figure of his neighbour standing in the window.

He stood for a moment thinking. What was it about Jack Culhane that irritated him so much? The man always seemed to greet him in a knowing way, as though he was privy to some secret of his. He moved through the gate into the garden and crashed into a dustbin hidden in the gloom. Charlie Sheehan was drunk. Oh, there was no doubt. He wouldn't deny it at all. After the amount he'd put away he'd be very disappointed if he wasn't drunk.

He looked up the garden. There was only one light showing at the back of the house. The bulb had gone in the toilet, he remembered, so he stood in the half-light of the garden and peed on to the weeds behind the bins.

A prig, he decided. That's what Jack Culhane was. A damn prig, nothing more. In the years they'd been neighbours he'd never had a drink with the man. Not one solitary drop together in all those years. Not even at Christmas. Kept his company for a bunch of cronies in town and one or two stuffed shirts in Blackrock.

Sheehan stepped out from the half-light of the wall and found the garden touched with silver. Beautiful night. Absolutely beautiful. There was a great crowd of stars out. Packs of them. He set off up the path which was becoming an ever narrower trail that fought a desperate battle with the weeds and border plants. He must do something about it. One of these fine days. God, what would it be like in summer if this was the state of it now.

He swayed as he walked. There was hardly any damn path left. He stopped for a moment for breath. He found he had to do that more often these days. He looked up. The full moon glinted on the roof slates. Damn it! What the hell was that? He retreated a few paces to try and get a better view. It was a hole and no mistake. There was a damn hole in the roof. No wonder the stairs had got wet the last time it had rained! He reckoned it to be about a couple of feet in diameter. Must have been those gales last year. They'd brought down trees the length and breadth of the country so there was hardly a road you could drive down safely.

He propelled himself forward again and fell in the kitchen door. Don't seem able to keep my feet tonight. Bockety, that's what I'm getting, bloody bockety! He weaved up the hall and opened the living room door. His family were in. His vast wife sat swathed in multicoloured layers. She didn't look up, but said hello absently. Her real interest lay in running her fingers over the layers of the chocolate box on the sofa beside her. His sons and daughters occupied the remaining chairs in the room. None of them moved. They greeted him after a fashion, if a slight raising of a paper or the flick of a finger could be called that.

His wife burst into song. Something loud and foreign. Italian he thought, but he wasn't too sure. She had taken to doing that lately. He wouldn't mind if she'd joined an amateur dramatics club or a choir, but she hadn't. Worse. She didn't have a note in her head. She had the formidable bosom of a diva and her gestures were wonderful, but the notes that came out would stop a dog fight.

He stood looking at her for a moment. The others only looked mildly put out. Except of course for poor Clare. Well named. If only that great and decent Order would take Clare off their hands. She sat there like a big bag of hammers. Hunched over. Her jaw always slack. She gazed at her mother

53

with a half smile, as if she wasn't sure if there was something to laugh at.

George glanced over from his place at the window, where he sat hunched over his accountancy books. May sat on the edge of a chair holding a mirror at arm's length and carefully readjusted a strand of hair. No doubt she had arranged to meet another damn bank clerk in the alley around the corner. Couldn't understand it, but she never brought the poor wretches in for so much as a cup of tea. Come to think of it, he only had her word that she was out on a date.

He picked up the late *Press* and rousted young James with a swipe – there was another ferret-faced pup in the making. The boy made way for his father with ill grace. How the hell did he get saddled with this lot, he wondered. As he adjusted the paper he smelt his hand again, and worse, saw. He excused himself and dived for the door.

In the bathroom mirror he found himself looking at a face that was beginning to look lived in. There was a sort of yellowness creeping into his moustache at both ends that was beginning to irritate him. Nicotine, the bloody bastard! Well, he wasn't going to give up now. He'd tried that once and it was a bloody disaster. He'd chewed right through his tie at work and had looked a right gobdaw on the train home. To hell with it! He dried his hands and noticed another black damp patch on the wall. Right in the corner where he could just see it. Why the hell didn't she tell him about these things so he could do something about them?

He noticed the towels were filthy, and made a note to tell Clare to wash a batch. That's all she was good for, really. She should be in a home, but they were so expensive.

He regained the living room and turned off the hall light. His younger son was back in his seat again, so he crossed over and hoiked him out of it by his ear. A quick crack on the back of his head sent him running, wailing, to the sofa. His mother included him in the aria she was still singing and clasped him to her bosom, shooting her husband a glare as she did so.

Bedlam, a madhouse. May as well not be here for all the notice they take of me. I should have stayed in the pub. Maybe Culhane would have showed up and bought me a drink. Really, when all things were taken into account, he didn't really like Culhane or any of his family for that matter. They were only culchies from Kerry, after all.

He turned to the paper. His wife continued to sing so that even James had to extricate himself from her folds and retire under the table to lie full length and read.

May suddenly rose and skipped across the room to him. For a second he thought he was about to be attacked. Then she planted a kiss on his head.

'Must dash to meet Gabriel,' she trilled. She had always been a triller. It had been charming when she was a little girl, but now it struck him as faintly ridiculous. Perhaps it was why Gabriel was the latest in a long line. They had all identified her as a triller and had gone their own way. She was through the door before he could mumble any admonitions about coming in late. Mrs Sheehan stopped singing her aria, only to sing 'Byee', and then popped another chocolate into her mouth. She stopped singing. A silence. Time to read the paper.

He stretched his feet towards the meagre fire. Sensing something, he looked down. Slippers. Damn blast it to hell! He was wearing slippers! No wonder he was awkward on his feet. Who wouldn't be with his feet in bloody slippers? Not only were they indoor shoes, but they looked as though they'd been out of doors and had had a hard time of it. They were stained and dirty and had chewing gum stuck to the toe. As he slipped them off he caught his wife shaking her head at him.

'I saw you go out in them hours ago. I was wondering when you would get around to noticing.' She picked up a magazine and flicked it open.

'There's a hole in the roof. Do you know that? There's a damn hole in the roof, you know! Saw it myself as I came in. Now what are ye going to do about that?'

She looked up at him.

'I'm perfectly aware there's a hole in the roof. Mrs Culhane was the first to point this out to me as I went about my business at Blackrock some months ago. She was followed, in no particular order, by Mrs Mac, Mrs Condon, Miss ffrench, and several Misters whose names I can't recall. Oh, and Mr O'Sullivan. But he's in the GAA, or should be judging by the cut of his jacket, so he doesn't really count.'

There were times lately when he really thought she had taken leave of her senses. She sat there now quite happily, it seemed to him. The house could collapse around this woman.

He was about to start an argument, but decided against it. They hadn't really spoken about anything for several years. He remembered that they'd argued about an election once. She'd taken the side of that communist Brown. He smiled at the thought. In those days they used to go out. That row had been in the pub with some friends. He had enjoyed going out, they both had. But in the last few years they seemed to have stopped doing anything together. He threw the paper aside and rose unsteadily to his feet. Bloody slippers.

'Under the tea towel in the kitchen,' she said without looking at him. He shrugged and crossed over to the drinks sideboard. He found a glass and poured a gin. The tonic bottle was empty, so he drank it down neat and its coarseness burned him. Funny thing was that gin always tasted so much better in a pub.

He went down to the kitchen and raised the towel. There were two slices of cold pork from the day before, some pickles and a pair of warmish boiled potatoes. He sat down and buttered himself a slice of bread.

He couldn't shake off the feeling of fragility these days. Nothing tasted quite right, either.

Mother put the bits of cardboard back into her bag and lit another Sweet Afton. Jack had always been like that, of course. From way back. As long as she could remember he hadn't the common sense of an ass. It had been a definite mistake to allow herself to be saddled with a brood of gannet-like children, but there you were. That was done. Of course, when she had the millstone firmly in place, then there was nothing to put a brake on his nonsense. Once they'd bought the place nothing would do him but to be parked in some bar in town surrounded by cronies, spending money as though he was the bloody Lord Mayor. At least he could have shelled out for a maid while you could still get one but oh no, even that had been beyond him. Beyond his drinking bill, more like! She'd been left to do everything and now you couldn't get a maid, except for astronomical wages.

Big Fella, she'd called him. She might have known that it didn't apply to his brain. People would know as soon as he set foot on the Avenue. They'd be beside themselves in their haste to tell one another. She wouldn't be able to set foot in Grahams again. She couldn't bear the thought of Mrs Graham looking down her nose at her when she went in. The children would have to take care of the local messages from now on. There was no other way for it. They'd all have to cope.

As she sat smoking, she mentally divided up the Avenue into friends and enemies, and was pleased that there were more of the latter. She had never cared for the area right from the start, and they had only come here at his insistence.

She wondered where they had all gone. Her dreams and ambitions. They had been buried under a mountain of soiled nappies. That she wasn't the first to suffer such a fate bothered her less than the frightful waste of it.

Here they were rattling around in this huge ramshackle house that needed a dozen repairs on each floor, and because of that stupid eejit they could hardly afford to replace a window pane a month. In the middle of winter, too. That was typical of his sense of timing.

She had meant to leave many times in the past. Just pack and go. But the children had closed off that escape. Ignoring him as much as possible was at least not too difficult. That was a point in the house's favour. As long as he kept to the front room she had hardly any need to see him from one end of the week to the next.

She looked at the nicotine stains on her fingers and resolved again to switch to filter-tip cigarettes. She spread her fingers before her. She liked her fingers. They were slim and delicate. They had played the piano when she was a girl. Not to concert standard, but passably well. Now they didn't have a piano and her nails were chipped.

At the first opportunity she decided she'd pop into the auction rooms at Blackrock and see if they had pianos in. If he could sit around scribbling all day then she could jolly well start playing music and he could go to hell. She'd get the money somehow.

She'd been impressed with him the first time she'd seen him. Was it in Cleary's restaurant, or not? She couldn't recall, but she'd been taking her lunch with friends when he'd come in with a crowd of fellows from down the Quays.

'Oh, that's the Customs crowd,' Deirdre had said to her. 'Steer away from them. They're a bit of a wild lot altogether.' Naturally she'd ignored Deirdre and had herself introduced. She wasn't even attracted to him at first. He seemed too quick with his smile. No, there had been another fellow there from down home. A small, handsome, dark man. They'd gone out several times together, or as part of a group from the office. It hadn't lasted long, though. The small man drank too much and never seemed entirely sober. It was not an attractive drunkenness, and she'd ditched him when he'd thrown up into the Liffey from Eden Quay.

Then she'd bumped into the Big Fella quite by chance in O'Connell Street. Oh, there was no doubt about it but that he had on a smart hat and pressed shirt. He was a cut above the other men she knew and he seemed to know his way around. Their progress around the town centre was marked by his effusive greetings, and he swapped remarks with a baffling array of men.

She recalled how much a part of the swing of things she'd felt as she walked by his side, and if he drank, he knew how to hold it. He got merry, certainly, but never in all that time did he lose control.

She found herself swept along from one restaurant to another, from the races to the fights, and to all the shows. It surprised her that she liked the fights so much. 'Kick him in the slats!' she'd scream, and then laugh uproariously at her own daring.

Whatever he was earning, he always seemed to have plenty of cash. It was always his round, and his friends thought the world of him. She had decided he was for her even before he'd called at her lodgings in an Austin Seven, and driven her out to Bray.

12

I saw Father one day in Blackrock a month after he came
home. A cold overcast day. Down the street came a vast herd
of cattle all heading for the slaughterhouse. This building looks
so innocent. It's just a cluster of tumbledown sheds at the end
of a cobbled lane. Inside. Now that's different. Here, out of
sight of the approaching animals, the floors are slippery with
blood which runs, foaming, into a central gutter. The men
who work there take pride in making sure that their freshly
cleaned white aprons become as bloody as possible in as short
a time. They are never disappointed.

Outside the cattle stand in the middle of the road and block
it. They take a leisurely look around them at the chaos they've
caused and stare curiously at the cars which toot at their
moos. The drovers don't rush them. They allow them these
last, fleeting moments. Why shouldn't they see the town before
they die? 'Poor creatures,' Mother says.

One by one they enter the slaughterhouse lane and waddle
along the cobbles. At the far end they're shoved and pulled,
one by one, into pens. That day I fancy that I actually see
the slaughter man raise an ugly iron mallet above a soft woolly
head.

Down at Grehans, the butcher, they wait for this fresh
consignment to come thudding on to the counters or be
hoisted on to damp, broad shoulders and carried through to
the cold rooms at the back.

As we cross the main street I see Old Grundy, the barber,
glance at his watch. He is thinking that Frank O'Shea, the
slaughter man, will be in soon for his usual trim. Whenever
they kill on a Thursday, Frank comes in to him. Frank kills

60

all over Leinster. What stories he could tell, but Grundy doesn't encourage him. He nips enough ears in his own working day without having the customers sickened by the slaughterer's tales of difficult bullocks. Grundy already has a reputation for being a bad-tempered man. Blackrock mothers regard it as an asset in a barber.

In James Grundy they had a man who stood no nonsense in the face of a tidal wave of crew cuts and DAs. What they didn't understand was that Grundy was really grumpy because he was angry with himself. He longed to be able to get through a morning without nipping an earhole and causing blood to flow.

At least once a day his scissors were guided towards a naked ear or cheek, as if possessed of a life of their own. There was little the poor barber could do about it. The scissor would seek out the spot and there was your daily nip for you. Grundy would sometimes feel quite ill with tension if the blades hadn't done their bloody work by morning. Once he'd nipped someone he could barber away happily but if he was knotted up with waiting then the tension became too much and his hair-cutting became very careless.

At times he wondered what was wrong with him. Perhaps he was fixated with pink flesh. He studied vampirism and bloodlust at night, seeking an answer. Once he sat up for five hours in a Protestant graveyard. All night. But nothing came of it except a fierce cold up his arse. He complained to his trapped audience for days afterwards. Waiting for Frank made Grundy brood about blood.

Mother and I watch the last of the animals being driven in by a young lad whose patience has run out. He lashes at them with a stick but his face is red with shame. We wander the streets. I know all the shops. Adult faces peer down at me and comment on my dimple. I never know what they're talking about and prefer to loiter on the pavement outside.

Suddenly I saw Father and am shocked by the sudden realization that I now know what unemployment is. It was odd seeing him there in Blackrock, a large, bearded man pulling on a glove while he stood on the steps of the library. He concentrated on the sky as though worried about the

61

weather. He had the air of a man who could go where he pleased.

I turned to tell Mother but she'd already seen him. Nothing was said but we both fell silent and observed him. Spied on him. Without saying anything neither of us wanted to see him.

Suddenly he came to a decision and set off down the village with a purposeful stride. We watched him pass, quite close to us, but he didn't see us. As he went he smiled at passers-by and raised his hat to two women on the corner. 'Well isn't he the one,' Mother said. 'Isn't he the one with the airs and not a brass farthing in his pocket.'

We turned and took the road home. I couldn't imagine a man so debonair and well known having no money. Only the week before he'd given me half a crown. All the way home I was nagged by the suspicion that Father just might be some sort of criminal.

13

Jack had seen them. Ellen and the young fella. Odd seeing his wife and child, standing in the street like that. As he came out of the library he'd caught a glimpse of her. The boy was pulling her sleeve but she'd stopped him. To hell with her. He would walk on then and go about his business. He twirled his walking stick very purposefully and walked quite close to them pretending he hadn't seen them.

He stopped by the cross in the main street. Its great antiquity made him wonder if Red Hugh had ever seen it. He wondered who had stood where he now stood. Every time he saw the cross it appeared to have altered slightly. In his mind's eye he saw it as a richly ornate Celtic cross with patterns and designs on it like those that were common in his history books.

The real cross was no more than a weather-pitted lump mounted on an ugly concrete stand. There was only the faintest trace of design left. The weather had moulded it over the years so that now it resembled a hunched cat. He fancied he could make out the suggestion of ears and whiskers.

No one locally, not even Miss MacEntee, could say precisely how it got there. She merely sucked air over her teeth and contented herself with saying that there was a great deal of telling behind that piece of stone.

The Normans were behind the cross. Strongbow and Raymond the Fat. People had told the story for so long, until they'd honed it and polished it so much that they felt it came from a book.

Everyone knew that the Normans had come over pretending to help Dermot of Leinster against his enemies, when all they'd really wanted to do was pillage and plunder all round them. They happily attacked friend and foe alike. They rode on iron horses and wore helmets and chain mail. The Irish scattered before them.

It reached the stage that people panicked at the very mention of them and fled. They abandonned everything to the steel-nosed ravishers. The Gaels packed everything into their cloaks and moved off across the bog land to the mountains. There they sought shelter from their tormentors. There they would stay until the storm passed.

But this time the storm didn't pass and those poor wretches were never to return to their lands because the Normans stayed put. Strongbow and Raymond were great collectors of anything that they thought they could sell. Whenever they came across a church or monastery they would race one another to get across the threshold first.

Everything of any value was loaded into carts and guarded by foot soldiers. The guards weren't afraid of meeting any Gaels because they were cocky and fat and lazy and usually drunk. They may even have been all those things on this particular day where Blackrock now stands.

Not that the guards were Normans. They were Flemings and they'd had their fill of Ireland. The climate was awful and the people were strange. They just wanted to serve out their contracts and get back to the English Borders or, better still, all the way home to Flanders. For all these reasons, people would say later, the booty train wasn't very well guarded at all.

The Gaelic Irish rose up out of the ground on the Main Street and fell on them. The Irish were led by a truly awesome warrior called Maolshoclann O'Byrne from the fastnesses of Wicklow. He tore into them with his double-edged sword and sent heads spinning in all directions. His men followed behind, howling like animals, and waded into the guards with pikes and swords. The Flemings were wiped out in minutes.

The Gaels stood triumphant over their enemies. They were good at ambushes. The carts were unloaded. In the last one they came across the cross. They couldn't see what the

Normans would have wanted with such a thing until Cormac Og O'Byrne pointed out that the cross had precious stones embedded in it. They went to work with their daggers and prised and levered the stones out.

Before they left Maolshoclann ordered that the cross should be placed on a boulder to mark the spot of their victory. This was done and the cross remained there for hundreds of years until people came out from Dublin to build there. They moved the stone from its boulder and rolled it into a field where it was quickly overgrown with weeds.

Not until the eighteenth century did Lorcan O'Toole stumble upon it after he'd decided to bring that piece of land under cultivation for his landlord. Not that Lorcan was any the wiser. He was merely the instrument. He rolled, heaved and levered the stone out of the pit it had settled in and brought it to light.

It was Alexander Lyle, a Presbyterian minister of ferocious conviction, who took an interest in it as he ate his midday meal nearby. Something about the shape of the rock interested him, and when he had finished his lump of fatty mutton and bread, he crossed over to it and began to scrape at it with his walking stick. Bit by bit, and now with a knife as well as the pointed end of his walking stick, he began to expose the design on it.

There was so much hardened mud, lichen and moss on it that it took him some time to work out that the stone was cross shaped. When he had done so, he shook his head in outrage at this relic of pagan popery and went on his way.

Local people, adherents of the old faith, set the cross back up as a rough shrine and gradually the village grew up around it. The centuries and motor exhausts had obliterated it until now it had become this hunched cat.

Father wondered how much of the story was true. People believed what they wanted to but there must be a grain of truth in it. Several stories had come together. As he put up his hand to caress the rough surface he wondered how he would put together the story of Red Hugh O'Donnell. He had hoped that some historical spirit might communicate itself to him through the rock.

Drawing pictures was one thing but he knew that he must tackle the writing sooner or later. He left the misshapen statue and sought the cool darkness of Dolphin's Bar to try and assess the real problem with O'Donnell.

14

While Father tried to write, Ireland was presided over by the tall half-blind Devotame, a leader accorded almost God-like status by much of the population. Like many such tribal leaders he was not a forward-looking man. Hampered by his poor sight and his advanced age, he was out of touch.

As the Everly Brothers and Tommy Steele crackled from radios, he imagined he led a country full of strong, straight young men and comely young girls who conversed in Gaelic as their ancestors had done. No one was quite sure how to disabuse him of this notion, but there were younger men flexing their muscles and growing impatient for their time. Young Lemass took over real power.

By the Bay the people had little interest in Gaelic unless mocked by a foreigner. In that case they would muster a few phrases and become stout defenders of Erse. At night, they would tune in to Radio Luxembourg and listen to a hit parade of American crooners.

In *Time* magazine, bearded rebels in peaked caps, routed the brutal Batista in Cuba and sent him packing. We saw them on the Pathé News in the Pavilion. Father approved of them and we played at being Castro in the Bug bush by the railway.

Liam made plans to go to England the following summer. He announced this, without any warning, one evening at tea. There was plenty of work to be had for a few months and everyone was doing it. Mother thought that was a splendid idea.

On clear, starry nights, people crowded on to the lawns and searched the skies for satellites. Sometimes they could see a speck of light moving slowly across the sky and they would cheer and everyone would feel that they were all part of something important. I started to read Jules Verne.

Being French, feeling French and living and breathing all things French. That's what Anne and Mary wanted to do. Oh, if only they could melt into the pictures in their magazines and become figures in a luxury advert for the Côte D'Azur!

Jean Gabin, Belmondo, dreamy Delon. What figures and what men! They knew how to light a woman's cigarette, hold a drink and order a meal. If only they knew men who wore trenchcoats like that. Gleaming white on a flickering black and white screen.

They went into town to see foreign films and if you closed your eyes on a spring evening and tried very hard, you could imagine O'Connell Street as a boulevard full of cafés and brasseries. The disappointment came when you opened your eyes. Then my sisters only saw hordes of men in their lumpen suits wearing tight, white shirts and their fathers' ties.

How they envied the Princess of Monaco, their own Grace, whisked away from them to a golden Mediterranean shore by a handsome prince. They collected all the wedding photos and felt that the marriage brought the continent a tiny bit nearer.

Every time they saw so much as an Eiffel Tower in a travel agents, they would hug themselves tightly and imagine the perfumed breeze of the boulevards where ladies would trip daintily by, dressed by Balmain and Dior, with a hand poised on their tight waists. Suavely Gallic men would accompany them with trenchcoats draped casually over shoulders. Handsome gendarmes would smile at them and touch their kepis. Everywhere, Citroens and Renaults, Gauloises and Ricard.

Those lucky few who had actually visited the shrine would be remorselessly squeezed of everything they'd seen or heard. They would go to people's houses to read *Le Monde*, over and over.

There was the French way and the rest. The rest varied considerably, but they were certain that the Irish way was worst. The country was teeming with bogmen so what other way could it be. You couldn't make ratatouille if your life depended on it.

But they were not solely concerned with fashion. Once, on a darkened winter afternoon, they sat gazing at a picture of Caryl Chessman. The news had come through that morning. Mother had entered their bedroom and had hovered above them. They'd been aware of her before they'd really woken up. They'd known something was wrong the moment they'd opened their eyes.

'What is it? What's happened?'

'I don't know how to tell you both but I'm afraid they executed poor Mr Chessman last night.'

'I knew it!' Mary burst out. 'I knew they would! Oh the cowards!'

They'd both wept loudly and Mother had stood uneasily at the door, excluded by their tears. She'd waved her hand and tried to think of something to say that might grab their attention and make them stop. 'We heard it on the radio about an hour ago but we didn't want to wake you so early.'

'That's just typical of them. They were scared of him because he was able to defend himself.'

The girls clung to each other and continued to weep. Anne managed a few words between her bitter sobs.

'It's so wrong! So wrong! He was innocent, he didn't do any of those things.'

Mother had thought to herself that her daughters would have plenty more unfairness to put up with before they'd run their course but all she'd said was, 'Well, as I said, we heard it on the radio but there wasn't much detail. Just that his appeal had been turned down and that they'd gone ahead with it at seven their time. The poor man. God rest his soul.'

Caryl would have died bravely, they were absolutely sure of that. He would have had more dignity than the governor and all his men. They sat on the edge of the bed and wondered what kind of priest would have been involved in something so wrong.

Downstairs Mother wondered what all the fuss was about. She addressed herself to me as she clattered about the kitchen.

'I mean to say no matter how charming a fellow he was, and they say he was, he was a convicted man, and that's what counts in the heel of the hunt.'

Father read the short report in the paper and said, 'Well, it's put an end to a lot of drawn-out codology.' The policeman in him liked a tidy ending.

That evening BB glided into my sisters' world from another planet. They were mesmerized by him and quite forgot the Red Light Bandit. BB undid the button of his dark suit to reveal the snow-white shirt to the full. He stood there in our front room, completely relaxed and at ease. Then he moved over to the couch and leant on the back of it between Mary and Anne. He smiled spendidly and spoke respectively to Mother, Aunt and Father.

In return they gave him their full attention. Liam was swiftly and unfavourably compared to him. BB had short, neat Brylcreamed hair with his tasteful tie and his dark, expensive suit. He was Bobby Darrin, Mr Nice with a hint of Mac the Knife.

Liam fingered the cuffs of his sports jacket where the threads were fraying and insisted on wriggling out to dangle. He felt hot and uncomfortable and was made to feel worse by the sight of his sisters glowing under the young god's radiant smile.

Though barely twenty, BB oozed success. He spoke of the future, of a different Ireland, a dynamic European country, that would shed its old ways like a flaky skin. All a fellow had to start with was a bit of capital. Ireland wouldn't give him that but he would never bow the knee and head obediently to some building site in Hammersmith or Wolverhampton.

Brazil. Rio! That was the place to be. Plenty happening out there if you knew what to look for. Naturally he'd miss Ireland but that was something you had to put behind you.

Did they notice the hint of steel in his eyes or was it just avarice? No, they didn't, because they were already on the streets of Rio watching the Carnival and the swirls of mad, bright colours. They sat at a pavement café and drank cool, long, utterly fabulous drinks with strange names.

BB left us that night, the adults in a romantic fog. The moon rode fat and high and the stars were reflected on the Bay. The family sagged in the front room, staggered by it all, thinking of Brazil. I fancied I could see my future in every moon-touched cloud. Every fold was a silver opening full of

70

hope and promise. No one paid my moody expression the slightest attention.

The rest of the evening we sat around reading books and comics and listening to Liam's records of Ella and Fats Domino. Every now and then the girls would sigh and Liam would snort.

Mary and Anne felt they would never rise above the utterly shameful as they shoved stuffing back into the jaded couch and struggled to turn the cover over another outrage.

How is it that he doesn't have spots, Liam thought. He dashed to the bathroom to check the underarms of his shirt. Nearly 1960 and they had Green Label parents.

BB danced the night away in the faded grandeur of the Royal Marine Hotel. He smiled his smile and walked a girl home to Glenageary. That Sunday he flew to London en route for Rio.

He grew fat in Brazil and his eyes said nothing. He patted his waist one day and decided that Rio was too hot and too far. Lisbon was the place to be. Europe. In his usual efficient manner he moved all his interests to a seedy run-down suburb in Lisbon and there he gave work to half-starved wild girls from the Alentejo. In return for a few escudos, their families could live above the breadline.

Old Man Salazar's got it sown up, he liked to say, when he came home to Dublin. You don't have anyone poking their noses in down there. The government sees to that. Should try the same thing here.

BB had been taken over by the slave trade. In broken Portuguese he would urge the girls to work harder and produce more. Any protest and it was out the bloody door with them. That's all they understood. If he needed any help all he had to do was give the police a ring. They knew him well.

He dined at the Shelbourne and the Gresham now and only passed the Royal Marine when he visited his mother. Mary and Anne never saw him again and they grew slowly out of his smile.

15

For weeks that December we scanned the skies to the north, trying to detect snow in the banks of low grey cloud that hung over the city. It must be snow. Everyone said so. People who really knew what snow was said that the weather was just like the winter of 1947. Back in that impossibly ancient time, it had snowed solidly, without let up, for a full six weeks. Six weeks! I couldn't imagine it as being anything less than Arctic. Glaciers in the Wicklow Mountains, ice two-feet thick on the Liffey and sheep dead in their thousands on the frozen blue hillsides.

Mr Clancy dies too. Frozen stiff in a ditch. They had to break his legs with a hammer to get them into the coffin and you'd never see a bluer face, not if you lived to be a thousand, my aunt said.

It took months for the snow to melt and some said it didn't melt at all up on the Kerry Reeks. The trams had stopped running at the top of the Avenue and the tracks of the main railway line had iced up.

We sat in our porch, my little friends and I, and thought about all of that. The snowballs, the sledding and the slides. To have had trams at all. Christmas cards of rosy-faced children filled our minds. Everything would be just so when it snowed.

I saw myself gazing out of my window at night. The cold would be fierce but thrilling in its intensity and the sky would be the deepest, darkest night-time blue. Over the Bay would be a swollen moon with every lake, sea and mountain range clear to the eye.

Shadows would stretch right across the lawn and down to the sea and it would be still and quiet. If you looked very carefully you could see a satellite. Nightly I craned out of my bedroom window expecting to see smugglers hauling for shore.

In my comics on such nights boys slipped out of their dormitories at English public schools. Armed only with a torch and compass they would foil the plans of lumpish foreign spies. The hero's uncle would turn out to be the head of MI5 and he would treat them all to a slap-up dinner at the Grand Hotel.

I saw myself as one of those chums. Secret missions by moonlight. I'd lie under the blankets and try to squeeze just a few extra feeble rays from my torch so that I could get to the end of another ripping yarn.

Every evening, before bed, we'd drift to the window and check the weather.

'It's very still,' Mother would say. 'Mrs Kennedy thinks it'll snow before long.'

'Well the temperature's gone up and that's always a good sign,' Father offered.

'I found it colder today than yesterday,' said the aunt. 'It had a real rawness to it that would go through you. Mrs Gibson was nearly murdered with it above in that big house of hers. Big barn of a place tis no wonder really.'

'Hot air rises,' Father said, 'and makes ice in the clouds which fall as snow. It won't stick here though, that's a fact. It never sticks near the sea. Salt. It's the salt that stops it. That's why they put it on the roads.'

'Well she had a fur coat wrapped around her today,' said my Aunt, 'so you'd think she was about to freeze up there and then!'

'It'll turn to slush,' Father said. 'Can't stand that! When it goes dark and filthy by the side of the road.'

'How do the Yanks put up with it?'

'It's snowing!'

'They must be made of iron to put up with those winters.'

'Here it comes!'

'I wouldn't give tuppence for a fur coat.'

'What?'

'Will it stick?'

'What about a white Christmas. That would be grand.'

73

'Why is this paper always such a bloody mess by the time I get it?'

'Real snow!'

We rushed out on to the steps. Everyone on the terrace was out. Miss James hobbled out on sticks. It was snowing. Thick white blankets of it pelted down, making the streetlamp flicker dimly.

For one magic Christmas Nature had decided to let us have a white Christmas but it made little real difference to the atmosphere among the adults. Mother still glared across at the Sheehans muttering venomously.

'Dressing up like God knows what, when they haven't a roof on their house. The cheek of them. It's a pity those lumps of children couldn't get out from under and turn a hand to something respectable.'

Her irritation was swiftly tranferred to Father who emerged at midday on that Christmas Day. He looked older since he'd come home from the office. I hoped there wouldn't be a quarrel. It didn't seem right to row ankle-deep in wrapping paper. Father wished us all a happy Christmas, gratefully accepted his gifts, and retired to the front room with a bundle of magazines tucked under his arm.

Later we all trooped into the dining room and shuffled awkwardly around the table which was filling up with plates of food ferried up from the kitchen. I rushed in.

This was an important dinner. An adult dinner and not to be missed. You could judge how much progress you'd made towards adulthood during the year by how much you were spoken to by your elders. More important still was trying to assess whether you'd been listened to in any way.

Glazed smiles and nods, or eyes that began to focus on some object behind you, were a giveaway. Worse again was the sudden interruption by another elder requesting some item that they could perfectly easily reach themselves. How obvious the move was when you turned back to find your listener engaged elsewhere.

This time as they sat themselves around the table, I stood back to take quick stock of the meal's likely progress. Father was still in the front room winching himself to his feet and

74

preparing to rumble through to join us with maximum fuss and bother. He had last been seen with a full bottle of port and was listing dangerously on the corners.

I could feel the tension in the others. They were muttering. A bad sign. The spiced round appeared – steaming, glorious and black. Something unique which only we ate as far as I could make out. Not for us the turkey. Father wouldn't have one. A phobia.

'They're rather dry you know,' beamed the Aunt.

'I'd rather find out for myself,' hissed sister Anne.

I concentrated on the steaming slice on my plate as the ancient turkey debate flared briefly at the other end of the table.

'I don't know why we're the only damn family in the country who never have a turkey!'

'He's so selfish about it. A phobia about birds! He's a big baby, so he is.'

'No one's forcing him to eat it. It's too much really. I'm sick of it year in year out,' Anne again, trembling with anger.

'Well, that's just the way of it. You know that. Just humour him today. Perhaps next year.' Mother smiled happily at them.

'What did you have for Christmas dinner?' a teacher had asked me. The others had all shouted out 'turkey'. I don't know why I hadn't done the same. 'Spiced round! Spiced round! What exactly is that then?'

I'd tried to explain but had got muddled when it came to the colour. Urged on by the teacher's mock-baffled face my classmates were in uproar. Damn them anyway! I liked the spiced round from Grehans. And roast pork. We had that too. They could stuff their stupid turkey.

Father duly trundled in and took up his position at the head of the table. He grinned happily at us.

'Boys, oh boys! Oh boys!' he said. 'Will you just look at all this!'

'Will you carve?' asked Mother. She did every year.

'Sure I will and glad to,' he replied, still beaming and sharpening the blade on the steel noisily.

'Really,' huffed Mary chicly, 'we could do with less of that. Father? Please!'

Father looked a little hurt but merely shrugged and began to carve. Succulent pink slices with black spiced edgings began to mound on the plate before him.

I looked around. My younger brother was happily mashing up a roast potato between glugs of lemonade but the older ones had taken up a defensive laager around the wine. I hadn't noticed the wine. This was a new and daring and definitely adult addition to the proceedings. Liam had produced a bottle, like a magician, from between his legs and had placed it on the table. Putting the corkscrew carefully to one side he showed the neck to the empty glasses of my sisters.

I caught Father giving the scene an eye, with just a hint of disapproval but it quickly faded when Anne caught his eye and coolly held it. My Aunt and Mother giggled but allowed their glasses to be filled. Father sat and received his with the quiet dignity of a man who rarely drinks but for whom this was a special occasion for which he would make a rare exception.

I watched. My brother and sisters sipped their wine with such little fuss that it was clearly an everyday thing for them and not an event to make a silly, gauche and country bother about. I twirled my glass between finger and thumb and contemplated the emptiness of it. Clearly I had some way to go.

Mother pursed her lips and swivelled towards Liam.

'And I'll bet this cost a shilling or two? Tell me now Liam. What did you spend on that wine?' she asked. Liam smiled, hugely tolerant.

'Just drink, Ellen. Sure you never know but it might do you good.'

'Mother, it's bought, let's leave it at that,' Mary said.

'Ah, for God's sake! I'm only enquiring. It's a free country.'

'Mother! We don't want to go into that just now. Christmas. Remember?' Anne raised her glass almost menacingly.

'A lovely drop of wine too,' Father boomed, holding his glass to the light. 'A fine Bordeaux claret.'

Liam considered this and then leant forward, tapping the rim of his glass with his finger.

'Would you like a little more meat, Davey?' asked my Aunt. She already had the meat skewered for my younger brother's

76

plate. 'Ah, go on, you can manage a bit,' she laughed, and laid the slices on his plate.

Liam looked on, with theatrical helplessness, at this interruption.

'A drink,' he went on, 'that has not changed substantially in over a thousand years.' He surveyed us and we considered what he'd said in quiet awe.

'Ha! And Arthur Guinness dares to talk about tradition!'

'Well, they're not exactly the same thing, Liam.' This treachery from Anne.

'I always thought you needed hops for beer,' said the Aunt, pursuing a potato relentlessly around the plate until she pinioned it and sliced it.

''Tis hops or barley or some such cereal at any rate,' said Mother.

Liam shook his head despairingly.

'A fine claret. Goes very well indeed. Very well!' said Father.

'I think the Costains used to have hops growing years ago,' my aunt added, frowning in thought. 'Tell me how is it that they can get the Guinness so dark?' she asked.

Liam jumped in. Things were sliding away from him. 'But the thing is a matter of culture. We see tradition in anything over a hundred years old. They were building Chartres during our Dark Ages!'

'Well I don't know who brewed it but I'll have another little glass,' said Mother proffering hers.

16

Now that Jack wasn't working every day felt like a holiday to him and he was disturbed to realize that Christmas Day felt no different from the others. He had tried to look forward to it but it just didn't feel the same. Last year he'd happily waded through the Grafton Street throng for presents but this year it had seemed a huge effort just to pop into the local shops. He left Mother, as always, to take care of the children.

When it came to the rest of them, he suddenly realized that he had very little money of his own. He hadn't dared to question finances in detail. He'd just ignored them as long as no catastrophe struck. He checked his bank account. There was exactly fifteen pounds and seven shillings in it. He withdrew five pounds and purchased a few items. A scarf for Ellen and then, as an afterthought, one for her sister. Liam had received a shaving kit and he'd given the girls some costume jewellery. Not very imaginative of him, he would concede, but he felt that they'd understand. They knew how wrapped up he was in his book.

In the week before Christmas he'd managed to complete several neat drawings to illustrate chapter headings. In addition he'd found an interesting magazine article about life in Gaelic Ireland in the time of O'Donnell. He'd taken many notes from it. These he'd added to his file.

The snow had helped, of course. As he'd stood on the step watching the thick, fat flakes cover the lawn, he remembered his own childhood in far off Cork. It had snowed when he was six and he and his father had gone to Mallow in the trap. It had been a terrible journey back because the pony kept slipping and the wheels kept sliding into the ditch. They'd had to get off and shove and push the trap back on to the road a dozen times. When they'd got home his mother had put him straight to bed. Later he'd heard his parents argue below.

'You fuss over him too much,' said his father and he imagined him by the fire, sucking on his pipe and warming his toes.

'I do not!' said his mother. There was anger in her voice. 'Only an idiot would drag a child out in this weather. That boy will be something, you mark my words, but not if you put him into an early grave.'

He didn't hear what his father had said. Here he was now, trying to be something. Pity that neither of them would see it. Buried years ago in a small graveyard near Mallow.

He poured himself another measure of port. 'Port out of Oporto port,' he was fond of saying. He liked a good vintage glass. Couldn't stand Ruby. Bloody woman's drink! He felt full and drowsy.

The meal had been pleasant but he was aware of the changes. Liam was a man now for the most part and one who was growing away from him. Bright boy really but inclined to spout a lot of pompous rubbish. Talking about wine when the young scut could barely hold more than a couple of glasses without rushing for the toilet. And Guinness. He was sure that Liam had never had a drink of stout in his life. The boy had the makings of a first-class bore if he wasn't careful.

The girls were another matter. Mary was fine but Anne was a snotty brat and no mistake. He could hardly believe that they had barely left school. Now they were all suits and office talk. Knew it all. He was a bit shocked by the wine but he had to admit that they'd handled it well enough.

That's what it would be like from now on. They would grow and set their own boundaries. He knew how they hated not having turkey but the very mention of the bird brought back awful memories of a night in Mayo with his head stuck down a dank bowl in the outhouse. No poultry! That was one bloody thing they wouldn't change. Not while he was alive! They could all go to hell but he wouldn't have a feathered beast in the house.

79

He was surprised to find his glass empty and poured another, larger one. He strained to listen to what was being said in the next room. He heard himself mentioned. Definitely. He'd heard the word 'Father', then something he couldn't catch and then a great roar of laughter.

So that was it. Now that he was out of the way they felt that they could make jokes about him. Well damn them to hell! He'd be the one to laugh when his manuscript was finished. As soon as everything had settled down in the New Year then he'd sort it all out and put on a spurt that would finish the thing.

He heard more laughter. This time it came from behind the chimney. The Sheehans were dipping into the sherry. Something sweet of course. He could see old man Sheehan carefully measuring out a small glass for each of them. He toasted the wall mockingly and thought viciously, By God I should have settled that bastard's hash when I had the chance!

There he'd been, sifting some papers, when he'd been handed a list of people suspected of breaking food quotas. Right at the top of the list, there was the quare fella's name. A bloody smuggler no less. Could have put him away for six months for that. Too soft. Couldn't do it to a neighbour. In the end he'd let it slide. But he made sure that Sheehan knew that he knew.

He enjoyed catching his neighbour's eye as he mowed the lawn and smiling a knowing smile at him. Sheehan could never return the look. At the time he'd wanted to interrupt some nice terrace gathering and denounce Sheehan but the moment had passed.

He hauled himself to his feet and crossed to his desk. He felt himself stumble a bit. He grasped the edge of the seat to control himself. He must never let the others see him drunk on family occasions. He knew Ellen destested it and the girls would be appalled.

He picked up a pile of his notes and sketches. Not bad for a few months work. January would be a good month. He had a good feeling about it. That's when his new life would really take off. A new year and a new life. All the nuts and bolts would gell nicely. Ah, then the mockers had better beware!

He smiled to himself and slumped back into the armchair. There was more laughter from the dining room. He could hear Liam's bass voice pronouncing. Then, in a lull, he heard the noise from Sheehan's again. An insistent, low, machine-like knocking. It seemed to be from their upstairs. Leaning forward to the fire he could hear it quite clearly down the chimney.

17

Stephen's Day came. The snow lay thick and inviting. Every household on the terrace stayed late in bed and curtains remained emphatically drawn. People only stirred slowly and reluctantly. Adults wandered about in a daze while we played with presents. In the kitchen people gathered in the warmth for tea and toast. Mother took up position at the cooker and glared in turn at the kettle and, across the yard, at the Sheehans.

'She's got a new bandana-type yoke on her head at any rate,' she said to us finally, and added 'Blast it!' to the kettle.

'Oh, Mother! For God's sake, what has that woman ever done to you?' asked Mary, as she buttered toast.

Mother shot her a pitying glance.

'Well, it's as much what she hasn't done as what she has, that agitates me.' She saw no understanding on our faces so continued. 'In heaven's name she and her damn crew have turned that place into a pigsty down the years. There's not a scrap of carpet on the floors, the front is all shot to pieces and there's hardly a roof on the place, which makes me spit. I don't care a fig what she does with her own place but sure if she lets the roof go then we'll have to put up with it. There's rain on our side as it is!'

Mary considered this.

'I know all that. But what's she ever actually, actively, done to you?'

Mother snorted.

'She doesn't have to do anything! She's just there. That silly scarf wrapped around her great fat head and singing all sorts of opera that she doesn't know the words of.'

'Oh, and you do, I suppose,' Anne jeered, over a magazine. 'Mrs Culhane the great opera buff. You can just see it, can't you?'

'Oh less of your lip you two. I'll have you know that . . .'

'We know. You did music at the convent in Killarney,' we all chorused.

'And ye needn't make a mockery of it either. You two with your little jobs, ye've a long way to go and that's a fact.'

The girls hooted with laughter at her annoyance. Liam came in and quickly assessed the situation.

'It is a rather appalling sound all the same.' He kissed Mother.

'Well thank you very much. At least one person agrees with me.'

'Crawler!' the girls jeered. 'All the toast's gone anyway!'

He only smiled and sat down.

'Well, she's a very active pair of lungs,' the Aunt said.

'But whether it's in tune is another matter. Wailing away over there and not a bother on her. She doesn't give a damn who hears her or what time of day it is. She just let's fly.'

As if to prove Mother right, Mrs Sheehan could be heard. Her voice hauled itself higher and higher before darting downwards alarmingly. Mother winced and we joined her.

Then I heard it. A faint scraping of a violin.

'Can that be Andrew?' Mother was amazed. 'On Stephen's Day! He must be crackers!'

We all moved to the front step. I noticed the footsteps across the lawn leading to where Andrew now stood. The snow came over his ankles. His violin was nestled comfortably under his chin and he was playing obliviously and gloriously, not minding the snow or us or anything.

They said people wept when he played and you could believe that listening to him there in the bright, white day. He came from a wealthy family, the Aunt said. Monied people from down Tramore way. The Aunt knew the story. Let her tell it.

His father had been a fox-hunting man. Ex-regular army. Andrew got the music from his mother. She was a sensitive

83

soul who'd absolutely no time for her husband's activities. They stayed married though, for show.

While the bold Major was out flogging his horse across the fields she was making sure that young Andrew attended his music lessons. Naturally his Majesty didn't like that overmuch and he used to try to bully, coax and cajole Andrew out for a hunt.

She moved between them and put a stop to that and told the Major that he could do as he pleased but Andrew was having his chance. Oh, she was very strong on all the arty things! Every weekend she packed the place out. Artists and poets and the like. A very fast crowd. All of them used to their own style of life.

The Major used to sulk at his golf club at first but gradually he crept home. It turned out that he quite liked the arty crowd once he'd had a few drinks to loosen him up.

He even knew a bit about painting though he always kept that hidden under his tweeds. He liked nothing better than to sit down with a whisky and listen to them chattering on about Paris and Venice and the like.

Mother knew Andrew's story, like she knew them all, but her sister told them better than she did.

Whatever it was now, music school didn't suit him one bit. He just lost interest. You could see it in the way he dressed. You would see him pass down the Avenue and he looked no better than a tramp. A holy show he became in no time.

No one knew why and all sorts of theories were advanced. Drink and women. The usual sort of things. Though he was always polite to people he knew.

The Major reverted to type and started to snipe away about how it had all been a waste of money and that he'd seen it coming. She told him to either shut up or clear off, which was brave of her in those days. So he did shut up because when push came to shove he was much too comfy with his glass of hot toddy.

Next the young fella disappeared himself off to London. No one could find out why or where exactly. Turned up working in a bank eventually and when he came home again he looked the perfect little bank manager.

He lived with his parents for a while but they died quite suddenly one after another. Andrew sold the house. Took the money and lives in some dive in town now. Gambled every penny away. Left the bank without a glance. Stole from them seemingly, but they couldn't prove it. You'd never guess it to look at him, such a meek little fellow.

'He's not as old as he looks, poor man,' Mother said. 'He can only be about forty-five though he looks ancient!' She gave me a shilling to give to him.

'He still plays well for all that,' said Liam. I dropped the shilling in Andrew's cap but he didn't look down. His eyes were closed and he was smiling.

18

The snow melted slowly and its thawing brought with it the promise of great changes. In January 1960 the city seemed to be full of young men, full of ideas, all wanting to get ahead. They wanted Ireland to be modern and efficient. They had extra bathrooms built in their houses and they bought second cars.

They all wore dark suits and went to clubs in the city. There they drank whisky and soda and made deals. Plans for economic expansion were discussed at every meal. With the Devotame tucked away up in the Park the way was clear. Not for them would there ever be dancing at the crossroads or storytelling around peat fires. The old man was out of touch. The way was clear now for younger men. Who cared who won the old wars? Their fathers had worked the farm but not them. People spoke of 'drive' and 'energy'.

That's what all the papers were saying. Father didn't believe it. These young fellas didn't know the first thing about it. Where would the money come from? They'd a lot to learn yet about the real world for all their suits and cars. Father didn't think much of the way they had shunted Devotame into a siding either. Cheeky young pups. They'd never suffered for anything that was their problem.

He rustled the paper angrily. Things were always being changed. Why couldn't these curs leave well alone? Now the bloody unions were sitting up and wanting their say in things that didn't concern them. And the bally government were listening to them.

He rose and checked the barometer. It had fallen. He tapped it. It didn't look good at all. Outside the slush clogged the gutter in a thick black goo.

That night hurricane winds hit. They blasted the water around the Bay in a foaming, snarling rip tide. Huge waves rose up, were wrenched up by sheer force, then gathered in a mass and flung down on the rocks beneath. Great gouts of water were shot in through the rocks and fissures and then exploded upwards – through the gaps – in towering geysers.

On the pier a stack of bright blue barrels were plucked from their pallets, the ropes sundered, and the lot swept into the Bay. They were strung out in a line towards Howth like pretty blue beads on a necklace. All night the tempest battered the house and pushed and pulled the old wooden shutters with their drumming.

Above the adult world Davey and I cowered in our bedroom, pushing flat against the wall and wrapping our blankets tightly and defensively around us. Far off, over the wastelands, dogs howled madly, cats shrieked and the rampaging gale screamed in the elms. Now and then there were ripping sounds and buckling sounds. Splintering wood and tortured metal. Tiles and coping, slates and chimneys crashed from their perches into basements and windswept streets.

We longed for some sound from below, some small noise from the distant adults. Dark flights of stairs separated us from the cosiness and warmth of the dining room. I shuddered to even think of that journey. The landing light hadn't worked for years and who knew what lurked in the tallboy.

'What's Da doing?' Davey's voice startled me.

'Writing a book.'

'What kind of a book?'

'An adventure one I think.'

'When will it be finished? Will he read it to us?'

'I don't know. Soon I suppose.'

'I'm scared. What'll we do if the Croglin Hall Vampire is in the garden? It was on the radio today so it could happen, couldn't it?'

Every little sound from below made us strain for something familiar and friendly. A door opening, light switches going on and off. Sometimes there would be a call for tea or the sound of a toilet flush followed by footsteps going back downstairs. Then it was just us and the gale again. Mother had rigged up an iron pole and had wedged it against the shutters to stop them blowing in but the wind still surged and buffeted it.

We knew there were legions of gargoyles on the other side of it. There were panes of glass missing, so it would be easy for them to get in should the shutters give. I could imagine them, perched on the guttering, drooling at the prospect of flesh. They were out in the storm biding their time.

Inside, the besieged welcomed the lights of every passing car like BP welcomed the relief of Mafeking. Those lovely, warm, human lights that ran across the ceiling before the car passed on into the night carrying its driver through hell to a safe house down the Avenue. How pitifully few they were that night as we lay, eyes open, in the dark.

Once before Liam had woken us on his late return and I'd asked him what would he do if threatened by the denizens of hell. Picking up a heavy copy of a collected Dickens, he replied, 'I'd throw this so bloody hard that I'd drop the fucker right where he stood.' We'd felt a lot better about things and had gone straight back to sleep. But that night there was no Liam, just the dark and the wind.

Far away across the Bay we heard the sound of a siren. Lonely and wailing, it went on and on and didn't stop like the one o'clock one. There was a desperate urging about this one, a note of alarm that seemed to be trying to warn the sleeping city. Only we could hear it! Outside I imagined the population, dead in the streets. The roads were blocked with bodies and cars. It had to happen sooner or later. That's why I'd built a trench out in the front when the Russians had invaded Hungary. Now, as the siren wailed on, I knew for certain that the Russians had landed in Cabra and had marched on Dublin in force. Most probably they'd made it easy for themselves by dropping poison and wearing masks. That was it. Did they know about it downstairs? Were they alive to know? I could hear footsteps. Heavy ones, strange ones, booted ones. The whole house felt foreign and full of menace. There was death and destruction in the air and still that cursed siren wailed into the night. The wind bent and twisted its note. Only that Sunday we'd flung ourselves on our knees and prayed for Russia. Moscow must have heard and now they were below in the streets wreaking revenge. Perhaps the troops in Collins barracks could hold the Siberian hordes long enough for the Americans to come.

Please, God, let the yanks come! It's Sergeant Rock with his battle-hardened Gyrenes! They'd see the Russkies off pretty damn quick. Oh, Jesus, there hasn't been a car for ages!

The siren ceased and just as suddenly the wind died. The house sighed with relief. There wasn't a sound in the house. Nothing moved. The room was darker than it had ever been and the landing outside was a darker, deadlier shade again.

That was it. We wrapped the blankets around ourselves and dashed for the door. We snapped on the room light and together we hurled ourselves down the stairs taking them three at a time. Our momentum made us fall and, rounding the bend of the last flight, all balance was lost and we took them in a pyjamaed, blanketed mass that crashed into the drawing room door. The door opened with a yank as though Mother had been waiting behind it. 'Jesus, Mary and Joseph are we to get no peace with you? March right back up those stairs this minute! This minute! Go on and be quick about it! Do ye know what time it is? Ye'd torment a saint. What time of night do ye call this to be horsing around?'

Voices from within the warmth called out words of patience and understanding but they were swept aside as were babblings about marauders in the streets outside. Mother was much more formidable and we quickly retreated. The dark room seemed much less menacing than the hallway below where Mother continued to hurl threats and abuse up at us.

The next morning the sea continued to fling huge waves over the sea wall. The railway lines were under water. No trains would carry their adults into town that day and there was an air of ill-concealed excitement among the family when they gathered in the kitchen.

Nervously I surveyed the neighbourhood from an upstairs window but there didn't seem to be any sign of the invaders. In fact all seemed perfectly normal except for the storm damage. There were branches down on all the roads and debris flying about in the high winds, but I couldn't bring myself to see it as the aftermath of a Russian invasion.

The Bay took all our attention that day. Breakfast was a treat and we sat with the family and ate a leisurely meal and soaked up the chat.

'The roof's off the Daniel's house and Slattery's lost a whole load of slates,' said the aunt, who was delighted to be sneaking a day off work. 'They're lying here and there all over the Avenue in smithereens. I saw the whole thing when I went for the paper.'

Their presence meant that there'd be a coal fire in the dining room from the early hours for people to sit and toast their feet and listen to the radio and read the papers. But that was for later as far as we were concerned. The Bay drew us out.

We raced across to the bridge and surveyed the heaving, grey sea. There would be shipwrecks and beachcombing for sure and maybe we'd get a raft on to the flooded railway lines and row to Blackrock? All across the Bay things floated and bobbed along, blown this way and that by the wind and the racing tides. We inched across the iron bridge as near to the sea as we dared and were sent shrieking back by cascading waves.

How we wished for a telescope to spy out the Bay, and see exactly what everything was that was floating. In books they always had one handy that could pick out the lettering on a packing crate and reveal that it came from somewhere far away and foreign.

The day brightened and smelt washed and everyone made a trip down to the sea and stood in awe and wonder at the power in front of them. Whole sections of the promenade had collapsed into the sea. Huge pieces of wood, parts of a ship, we were sure, were being flung on to the beach with every wave. Easy to see how troopships had foundered here in times past. The rocks awash with red-coated soldiers, soggy and dead.

Father had come with us and as we watched the seas he produced a notebook from his overcoat pocket and began to make little scribbles and notes. Once in a while he would stand, lost in thought, and chew the end of his pen. Then something would occur to him and he would jot down something carefully then look at it. His lips moved as he read what he'd written. He looked old to me, there on the shattered promenade, and I wondered what age he was. But the idea made me nervous and I shrugged it off.

Besides I was much too busy. All along the shore there were treasures begging to be investigated, and we raced from one discovery to another, my brother and I, each of us anxious to be the one who would find the bloated blackened corpse of a wretched Lascar on Seapoint beach. Finding none we made do with a swollen sheep. The adults, Liam among them, held their noses and walked on. The Aunt said, 'Poor thing.'

That day we found enough wood to float a whole navy of rafts but our eyes were always on the bobbing blue drums drifting miles out to sea. If only they'd suddenly be caught in a kindly current and hurled back on our beach, then the raft that summer would be brilliant. We could sail anywhere and do anything. We would surge ashore at Maretimo and anni- hilate our enemies. But it was not to be. The barrels continued their meandering way and fetched up on a beach on the other side of the Bay, where a group of young fellas swooped on them, and turned them into the best summer diving platform that had ever been seen in that area for years.

A chest figured high on our list of most desirable flotsam and we were sure that day we'd be lucky. After all, the sea was full of yachts, and didn't any half-way decent captain know that you always kept your maps and a massive knife, compass and brass sextant and stuff nautical in a good stout chest? I never understood why we were always denied this simple token of friendship by the sea. We spent so much time in it and by it that I felt we'd earned it.

Then, for a heart-stopping moment, there it was. An oblong wooden shape in shallow water. With adult warnings to take care we swarmed in and dragged it out. The word 'Copen- hagen' was stencilled on one side but our delight was quickly doused as the box was empty, only had two full sides, and had probably never held anything other than bacon. Enraged at yet another insult, we bombarded it with stones.

The adults had gathered in the shelter of a Martello tower and saluted other groups of walkers. The talk was of storms.

'God, it would blow you right off your feet,' Aunt shouted, hanging on to her headscarf. 'I've never seen the like of it for years.'

'You have to kind of lean in to it,' said Liam grinning. 'The thing is exactly like sailing. You have to sort of tack your way along.'

The Aunt gave him a look but said nothing.

'Oh, there's been plenty worse storms than this. Plenty worse,' Father said with the air of a Polar veteran. He shuddered at the memory of a drowned face. 'Nineteen hundred and forty-two. Yes, about then. Might have been forty-three, now. Whatever. Well, there was a night of wind and storm then that makes this look like a little blow. Right across the south of Ireland it hit. Absolute bloody devastating it was.'

'Oh, I remember the one you mean,' said the Aunt, 'that was the one that Peggy Mike's son below in Glin broke his leg in.'

'The very same, the very same,' Father said, a little impatiently. His sister-in-law had a habit of taking over his best stories before he'd even warmed up.

'Fell out of a pony and trap dead drunk and broke his leg just like that,' she laughed at the memory.

'During the storm or what?' asked Liam.

The Aunt looked surprised by the question.

'Well now, I'm not sure about that. It might have been. Around the same time anyhow.' She laughed at their exasperation.

'There was hardly a house between Macroom and Cork that didn't have its roof damaged that night,' Father ploughed on, 'but the thing I remember most was the hedges and the fields. By God, they were flattened out, so they were. There was hardly a blade left standing, and there was more hedge in the road than there was in the ditch.'

'I hear that a horse got swept out to sea down in Wicklow,' the Aunt added happily. 'That's one of the strangest things I've ever heard of.'

'Oh, it would be quite all right,' said Liam, happy with facts. 'Sure, a horse could swim a good twenty miles, no problem at all. I mean, provided the beast was in good shape and didn't try and make it to Wales, it should have been all right.'

'What even in these seas?' The Aunt didn't look at all convinced and try as she might she could not recall Liam ever having been on a horse. Liam seemed to only just notice the waves and for a moment he wavered.

'Yeah. It's a bit rough all right. But they are powerful swimmers.'

'How the hell did a horse come to be by the sea in this weather anyway?' Father asked, tetchily.

'Well now, I couldn't tell you that at all. Maybe it got out from its field somehow and wandered off. There's plenty of fields by the sea anyhow.' The Aunt turned her gaze down the coast towards Wicklow as though trying to picture those very fields.

'It's a very wild class of a country Wicklow is. Terribly bleak in parts,' she said, 'you could imagine anything happening down there.'

'Oh, they say there are lost tribes all over the place in Wicklow. Just turn down any un-signposted little valley, and you'll run into people claiming to be the High King of Ireland,' Liam put in.

'That was another famous storm when Art O'Donnell escaped from Dublin Castle in the fifteen whatever,' Father said, seizing his chance. 'Froze his toes right off, so it did. They made their way through one of the worst blizzards on record to Wicklow. But he lost the toes. Snapped right off like icicles so they did.'

I tried to imagine toes falling like glass on the ground.

'Is that a fact? I never knew that, now,' said the Aunt.

'Happens all the time in the Arctic,' said Liam seriously.

We turned for home and the fire. Along the way I scanned the Bay hoping for the sight of a horse's head ploughing slowly along offshore. Maybe it had gone to Wales.

19

The following day the Bay was covered with thick cloud. The wind didn't abate and the rain drove into the faces of the children as they struggled to school.

People kept to the walls as they fought their way about with their heads bowed into the gales. Some said the weather led to a great straightening out of old scores and crossed lines because people couldn't look up and avoid one another. Enemies walked into enemies and had to say something rather than look stupid. Arguments were settled and old slights made better. But if that was a good thing then it was a rarity.

No sooner did the fierce winds die away than the frost hit. So hard that a nightwatchman was killed when a lump of ice fell from a roof above his brazier and crushed his skull into his overcoat.

The young rushed to ponds and lakes, despite warnings, and were drowned by the dozen as they fell through. The old stayed imprisoned in their homes, hoping that someone would remember them and run a few errands. The poorer ones turned blue and died where they sat huddled by an empty grate. There was lots of work for the Vincent de Paul.

At first the loose slates on the Sheehans' house were barely noticed among the general air of dilapidation that their house always wore. The rooms at the top were hardly used since George had moved into town. Poor Clare didn't mind in what part of the house she slept, for her needs were few. One day she had simply gathered up her bedding and clothes in her long arms and had colonized a room, where she'd cleared out a corner and set up house.

The rest of the Sheehans were barely aware of Clare's existence, save at mealtimes, when she was a mumbling presence who served them. Up above she surrounded herself with the many little objects that she'd collected over the years. There was a whistle that she'd kept from her brief stay in the Guides. She liked the sound it made. She had a small shakey of Lourdes. It made such a lovely snowstorm around the Grotto that she could hardly resist taking its smooth roundness in her hand and shaking it over and over. The blizzard in the glass was so real that she sometimes found herself shivering.

By her bedside, among her bottles of medicine, she had an old photo of herself taken on the front lawn. As she looked at herself, she felt her shoulder. There was no sign of the hump in the photo. In there, long ago, she'd stood straight. Sometimes she would look at it and shake her head, puzzled.

Her father would say, 'Clare's been looking at that damn picture again. I wish to God you could get it off her some way. She's only making herself miserable.'

Mrs Sheehan, to whom this was addressed, would just smile at the ceiling and reply, 'Ah, let's leave the poor girl with it. Sure she's little enough to comfort herself with now that she's grown.'

Charlie Sheehan was not convinced by his wife's attitude but knew that he would never get around to doing anything himself about it. 'Well I don't think that any good will come of it. Any good at all. She just stares at it all the time and it only upsets her or gives her funny notions.'

Whenever he thought about his daughter too much, Charlie Sheehan shivered. Could this big, slow crookback be a daughter of his? He found that he couldn't stop thinking about her hump. He imagined it, bare and naked to the world, on a bright, sunny day. At the beach maybe. He pictured a great white lump looming over his daughter's shoulder and the image made him go weak at the knees and his stomach to lurch alarmingly. He knew this was wrong but there it was. He couldn't help it. He had always been that way from childhood. He'd never been able to ignore physical disability. That Clare was his daughter only made things worse.

He opened the cupboard and poured himself a large Cork dry gin and added a touch of tonic as an afterthought. They should have had the girl put in a home years ago. He went into the hall and stood at the foot of the stairs. It suddenly occurred to him that he hadn't been to the top of the house for over a year. He would have to go there soon and check the condition of the place.

It was Clare's area since George had left. He didn't like to intrude. He fought down the feeling of dread at what he might find up there. How little he knew about her. She may as well have been an alien for all he really knew about her daily life.

That winter was the worst the terrace had suffered according to old Mrs Leeston and her memory went back to the previous century so it must have been a pretty dire winter indeed. The Sheehans huddled around the fire in their front room or sheltered in the kitchen. Their pinched faces flitted from time to time at the windows and there was smoke from one of the chimneys. Apart from these small signs it was hard to tell if anyone lived there at all.

Neighbours noticed that there seemed more holes in the upstairs windows than usual. Helen Nunan said that she hadn't seen them in the shops for a fortnight and wasn't it quare the way the weather was affecting people's habits. It didn't need weather for the Sheehans to be quare, Mother said.

She could have sworn that she'd heard Clare singing one dark afternoon as she'd passed down the Avenue. Quite a good voice. Light like, but good. It was what she was singing that caught the attention; Gaelic definitely. Something old that had a sad quality to it. She couldn't tell where the voice had come from except that it had been upstairs somewhere. She'd stood on the pavement a while. As the tune faded she fancied that she had seen a face look down at her from an upstairs window.

Spring and a real thaw finally came and freed them. First with a drip and then with a torrent. The country sank under the waters of it as the rivers and lakes flooded out across the plains.

'Thank God it's over, that's all I can say.' Sheehan stood on the step, watching the sea. The sun was shining and the fresh wind blew masses of light, white cloud down the coast. The Bay had a strangely bright, clean look as though someone had been busy with whitewash. Blinking in the unaccustomed sunshine the residents of the terrace emerged from their houses and, on their front steps, greeted one another, happy that their ordeal was over.

Mr Sheehan was happy with himself. George had sent home twenty pounds, five of which nestled snugly inside his jacket. Plenty of money in the accountancy line. There seemed some chance that May had finally found a young man to marry though how she'd managed it during that winter he couldn't say. That only left James, and his school days were numbered. He relished the idea of a walk down to Dun Laoghaire and the sinking of a few pints. He felt he'd earned them for being cooped up for so long.

May giggled and edged past him on the step. She was wearing a light cotton frock with a floral pattern and a cardigan draped over her shoulders. 'You'll catch your death going out like that. It's only a thaw, not a bloody heatwave!'

She made no reply but put her hand up to her mouth and giggled again.

'Mad as a bloody hatter!' he thought to himself. 'Pity the poor eegit she's managed to take up with.'

'I'll be fine, Daddy. Really. Don't be such a silly old fusspot. Oh, what a lovely day!' she sang and twirled her skirts. Then she turned and skipped away around the corner like a young child. As he watched her go he frowned. There was something unbalanced about that girl. May had a kind of manic edge to her that bothered him. He should talk to her sometime, if he could manage to get through her silly little girl act.

He went back into the house to get his coat. As he did so there was a deafening crash as rotting roof timbers gave way and crashed into the rooms beneath them. Ice, slates and wood whistled past where he'd been standing and hurtled into the basement. He felt his heart erupt so that he thought he must be about to have a seizure. His face drained and his knees gave way. He slumped into a chair in the hall.

'Jesus, Mary and Joseph what the hell was that?' his wife called. He couldn't answer for a moment.

'Charlie, have you gone deaf? I said what the blazes was that?'

'How the devil do I know,' he snapped at her angrily. 'All I know is that it was very nearly the end of me, whatever the hell it was.'

She appeared wearing a turquoise towel around her head and carrying a long cigarette holder. It occurred to him that she didn't smoke.

'It's the roof so it is. Go up now for heaven's sake and see that we're not all in mortal peril.'

He cursed under his breath but did as she asked and mounted the stairs. Clare was standing on the first floor landing with her hand on the banister and her mouth hanging open. He supposed that they should be grateful that she wasn't hurt. He brushed roughly past her. At times she annoyed him intensely. Stupid great lump, she always seemed to be in the way. As he turned to mount the final flight he saw the end of his house and all his dreams of a quiet life.

There was a great gap in the roof. He could see clear through to the sky and he could see fluffy white clouds scudding by. There was water running somewhere. From a back room clouds of dense, choking dust began to obscure the sky. The water tank balanced precariously on a wardrobe with the water inside it slapping against the side like a drum. A steady avalanche of black sludge advanced down the stairs towards him. It oozed its way pleasingly over each stair.

'Ah, for Jasus sake! This is beyond the bloody pale so it is. Beyond the fucking bastarding pale!'

'What are you saying?' Mrs Sheehan called from way below.

'The house. The bloody house is fucked. Completely fucked. It's a bombsite up here. A bombsite.'

He backed down the stairs. There was nothing for it but to wait to be engulfed by the black wave of sludge. As he stood, stupefied, it occurred to him that the carpet hadn't been cleaned for years. After this it would hardly matter he supposed. From where he stood, clutching the banister, he saw Clare emerge again from her room and ascend towards the wave of muck. She reached down and dipped her finger into the blackness of it and then examined it carefully. She gave a strange little snort and smiled her lopsided smile down at him. Then she went back into her room.

The damage done to the Sheehans that winter proved irreparable. The family funds had run very low down the years. Sheehan's pension was insufficient to cover the costs of the disaster. Gradually, one by one, the family folded their tents and made an orderly withdrawal to the rooms that were still habitable.

In the evenings Sheehan sat huddled in an old leather armchair and wrapped a rug around his legs to try and keep out the draught that sang in every corner of the house. The place sank in on itself as timbers rotted and beams sagged. More slates fell and the boiler had to be held in its moorings by an assortment of planks, each nailed to the one before it and the last somehow attached to the wall by rope.

Cold spring winds howled through the house night and day. They shrieked in through the roof and ripped their way into every room like some demented, perpetual banshee. The wind paid no heed to the season because the inside of their house remained frozen and wet. The wallpaper soon gave up trying to cling to the damp walls and fell away in great folds. Pigeons moved into the loft in huge numbers and their cooings and billings could even be heard above the wind.

Every night the Sheehans gathered in the front room while their father opened the bureau for the ritual of examining their assets. Rolls of scroll and old bonds were taken out and they sat around them discussing their value.

The beautiful copperplate writing was deceptive, for all of them were worthless. Anything of value had been sold years before. They rowed amongst themselves, anxious to ascribe blame for the disappearance of the family fortune. But it was half-hearted wrangling for they knew full well that there had been little there in the first place. None of them had the heart for a full blooded dispute. Mrs Sheehan fell silent and sang little for a while. The rest cursed quietly and drew closer to the fire.

20

'Tinkers. That's what they are. Just like tinkers the lot of them.'

Mother stubbed out her cigarette in the sink and poured boiling water into the battered kettle.

Across the yard icicles still hung, despite the thaw, from the Sheehans' kitchen window. Their window was steamed up and Mother could not make out what was going on behind though she stood on tiptoe and strained this way and that.

'Gypsies, Mother,' Liam said amiably. 'Surely they can at least be gypsies. After all this is the south side of town.' He smiled at his own joke and shook the paper out.

'Well, some class of travelling people or circus types. I don't know what you'd call them when you see her out with her hair done up in that bandana.'

'And you can hear her warbling away and not a bother on her,' the Aunt pitched in between mouthfuls of toast.

'I'll give her not a bother if there are any more leaks through on our side. Tis a pity they don't all shove off and live in a tent. As it is there's no peace from them.'

Mother had little time for the troubles of the Sheehans. As far as she was concerned they had brought it all on themselves by their careless attitude to everybody and everything. Liam's contributions irritated her containing, as they did, a faint ridicule of her anger. The girls were no better and were always trying to pin her down and get her to explain why she disliked the Sheehans so much. If she was honest with herself she would have admitted that she had lost track of what it was that annoyed her about the Sheehans. Thirty years of living beside them for a start. Just the sheer Sheehanness of the view out the kitchen window. Their grinning, silly faces at the window every time she glanced across. The fact that they never seemed worried that their house was falling down around them grated as did the much more serious fact that they didn't care a fig what happened to their neighbours' houses as a result.

The very first day they had moved in next door Mrs Sheehan had borrowed a pair of shears to clip a bit of hedge. They had not been returned nor had the blasted woman ever mentioned them again. The sheer effrontery of it still rankled as though it had happened the day before.

As if that were not enough, there had soon followed another incident which confirmed her suspicions about the Sheehans. She had come out one morning to hang some washing and had found the remains of several bottles of spirits lying by the wall evidently flung there by someone on the Sheehans' side. Later she'd seen Mr Sheehan placing a bag, clinking with glass, into the bin. There it was. The Sheehans were thieves and drunkards.

Their children were a strange inbred crew who never joined in anything but were always on the sidelines. They were the sort who always urged the others on but never let any blame attach to themselves. She'd seen them herself. Slyly suggesting that one of the other children get up to some piece of mischief and then looking saintly when the storm broke. They got their shiftiness from their parents.

Gypsies indeed! She was getting fed up with the way her own children were beginning to snipe at her. Liam, in particular, had a way of making fun of her while pretending to agree that was intensely annoying.

She rummaged in her bag and produced her collection of used cigarette packets. They were getting out of hand, she thought, as she spread them on the kitchen table. There must be a bit of card around somewhere that she could use to transfer these on to.

She began to run a pen up and down the columns of figures. It didn't look too good. There were quarterly bills to pay and there wasn't a damn thing to pay them with. The house seemed to eat electricity and the children were like locusts at the table.

Her sister could be relied on but her pay had its limits. If only there wasn't the ruddy mortgage to pay. She would never be done paying it off. There were times when she wished they'd never moved into this great big cavern of a place.

His idea, of course. Had to have a house to impress people. It never crossed the poor eegit's mind what it cost to run. And then to go and pick a draughty old pile like this! She heard a stirring. It was him moving about the front room.

He would be dug-in in there with a great pile of books and not a care in the world. Nothing could rock him. He had gone through the Christmas as though he'd been made head of the civil service. He didn't seem to notice the reduced rations they were on and she'd had to squeeze her sister to boost the presents when she saw the wretched offerings he'd appeared with. Oblivious to everybody and everything.

A cheap scarf. A common thing bought off a stall, with pictures of horses on it. It was in her bag buried under fags and keys and tissues and there it could stay as far as she was concerned. It would make a good duster. What kind of country was it where she felt as though she were bound with barbed wire to a man she'd once imagined she'd loved? Even as she thought of this she dismissed it as dishonest. No, she'd never loved him. She'd fallen for his suit and salary and she didn't suppose she was the first country girl to do that.

A thought crossed her mind. Maybe, just maybe, he might be on to something with this book. What if he were to write something that actually sold? He was boastful enough at any rate. He'd never been short of little stories and he was a wordy basket for sure. Someone had to write, so why shouldn't it be Jack Culhane? Mind you, she'd be damned for a heathen before she'd take any interest in his activities. Not directly at any rate. But they might be worth keeping a weather eye on.

Funny that she only really thought about the two of them when the family had gone off out for the day. Usually there was too much noise and distraction to give Jack much thought. Now in the gloom of the kitchen she was alone. Her sister had just left and Liam had vanished upstairs.

It was at times like this that she wondered if this was all there was to it. A squad of kids, no money and a husband

102

who came running home from work like a child bullied at school. The worst of it was that he'd never be able to see it like that. All he saw was what he wanted to. He was the hero who'd taken a brave decision to go it alone and follow his mission, not a first-class gobshite who'd packed in a perfectly good job for some flight of fancy. She thought of her grandfather dragging them up and down the country in pursuit of wealth. All he'd left behind was a frail old lady without a penny to her name for his daughters to look after. The Irish produced some spectacularly selfish men for the women to cope with. She put away her accounts and stubbed another cigarette out in the sink. Quietly she went up into the hall and along to his room. The door was ajar. She could hear faint movements inside. She put her head around the door.

He was sitting at the desk in the window. Light streamed in and bathed the scene with a warm glow. There were piles of books everywhere and piles of writing paper. He had his back to her and was hunched over, busily occupied with something on the table.

She came up behind him. She didn't creep so as not to startle him. He always made an enormous fuss when he was startled. She bustled in and swept up the newspaper that he'd left on the sofa behind him. He did not look up but just grunted.

She folded the paper. She was behind him now. She peeked over his shoulder. Still he didn't look up. He just shifted position slightly. As he did so she saw the page he was working on. He was drawing a picture. The man had come home to draw pictures!

He, for his part, had said nothing to her. He saw no point, if she was going to pursue this ridiculous vendetta. Much better to opt for a period of phoney war, and surprise her with a finished product at the end of the day. She would never be able to understand the complex processes by which a full novel, a piece of creative fiction, was brought into the world. She'd always been an impatient woman, well now she could just stew as far as he was concerned.

It felt good to run these opinions through in his head. It was as though he had never thought of taking up an extreme position on anything before, for fear of having to go into complicated explanations, but now that he'd set his radical course, he found it exciting. There was something rebellious about him. He'd started his own little war in his backyard. For the first time in years he felt that he was doing something that he, singular, wanted to do. He couldn't remember a time when every decision hadn't depended on the family. Revolved around the house. The great house that he'd bought with wonderful plans of filling it up with civilized people and good talk. Instead the Victorian building had filled up with screaming, demanding children.

Then there was her sister. She'd been installed, and by the time she'd finished he no longer felt that the house was his. The speed with which the children had arrived, one on top of the other, had left him feeling panicky and trapped.

There were nights when he'd left work and gone for a drink with the lads in the office. A group of men with pints in their hands gabbing away a few hours in harmless banter. Then the children had arrived. Pride and a sense of achievement had accompanied the birth of Liam. The others patted him on the back, bought him drinks and said what a grand fella he was. He'd put on his serious face and talked about responsibility. He smiled when the others ribbed him when he put on his hat and coat to go.

Then the girls had arrived. Time had betrayed him, for when he next noticed it appeared that he had a large family. He could hear the house from the station. Every room and stairway echoed with roars and shouts, idiotic rhymes, threats, fights and smells. The milky, full smells of children growing.

Then one evening it had come time for him to leave the pub and he hadn't. He'd stayed on. He remembered that the others thought it was a huge joke. Good old Culhane wouldn't be done down by life. Another pint had appeared at his elbow. He'd downed it greedily, taking in the approval of the others. Only Healy had shaken his head and not smiled.

After that it was easy. She'd said nothing when he had arrived home. Well, if that was all there was to it he couldn't see what the fuss was about. In fact he got the distinct impression that she wasn't all that pushed about what time he got home. Provided he didn't make a production out of looking for food, all seemed well.

His children seemed to grow up perfectly normally without him in close attendance and his wife was, if not delirious, then no worse off than many others. After all he wasn't the only man who was uncomfortable with small children. It wasn't unusual, he told himself.

Gradually it got to the stage where he was first to the pub every night. He would stand up at the bar and get a round of drinks in. He saw the others exchange glances when the clock struck nine but he ignored them. He felt their reluctance when he suggested a steak house dinner, but he slapped them on the shoulders and jollied them along.

He missed those nights and at times like this he cursed himself for a fool for jacking in the job. He didn't know how long the government would keep paying him. He had just that morning intercepted the mail. It was just as well that he had. There was a letter from the Department which informed him, very clearly, that as of receipt he could consider himself on half salary until such a time as the Department decided what course of action to take. That was bad news and he certainly wasn't about to share it with his wife. Time to wheel out the tame doctors and make sure that this time they were convincing. He folded the letter and slipped it into his jacket. Far off he could hear the noises of a Hoover as she worked her way down the stairs.

He gazed out at the bright, cold day and thought again of those pint-filled evenings in town. Even Hennessy didn't seem such a little bastard from here. Whelan and Moriarty called in from time to time and that made up for it a bit. But he did miss the whirl of town, the sense of activity and purpose. Besides, Tom and Bill still worked and only popped in when they were passing.

He turned back to his manuscript. He shoved the drawing to one side and read through a few pages. It pained him to admit it but he was growing just a little weary of Red Hugh O'Donnell. The man didn't appear to have done much but raid his neighbours for cattle and feast week in, week out. There was no doubt that he was a brave resourceful leader, all the books he could find said so. The trouble was that that was all they did. They cited very few specific instances of O'Donnell demonstrating any qualities at all. He was always O'Neil's loyal ally.

Despite all his notes it was proving difficult to make this man come alive on the page. He thought about ignoring history altogether and going back to the time of myths and legends. That would be easier, he thought, because then he wouldn't have to worry about some know-all poking his nose in and saying that this or that or the other thing couldn't have happened. After all, if he wrote that Queen Maeve wore a beard, then who could contradict him?

History was a trap. The Irish were too bloody obsessed with their own past. According to some the chieftains were saints. Catholic martyrs in constant struggle with the English invader. To listen to some people you would think that the northern Earls never so much as farted or if they did, then it was through talcum powder. He knew all this. He was determined to write something a little different, dangerous even. It was one strange distraction that was proving the problem.

He had begun to think about the office. Amazing as it seemed he actually felt a twinge whenever he imagined them all sitting at their desks. Healy and Hennessy, Mrs Fitz and the rest. There was the gossip and the papers and the happy lunchtime pints. He felt out of things. Adrift out here in the suburbs. There was nothing for it.

He went out into the hall. He could hear her hoovering away on the landings. He put on his thick coat. Quietly he went into the kitchen. Rooting about in her sack he found the purse and extracted some money. If he hurried then he could get the two o'clock train into town.

21

'Glamour Boy's here!'

We ran to the gates of the terrace and watched the figure on the bike hurtling down the hill towards us. His Australian bush hat was set back on his head and his feet were off the pedals and sticking out each side. 'Yeeeeeeehahh!' he roared at the top of his voice.

It must be the end of winter if 'Glamour Boy' was here. He'd wintered with a charitable order and didn't go abroad on his priest's bicycle until he was sure that winter had gone. The war had scrambled his brain but his sense of season was unimpaired by the shells at Ypres.

He didn't look right or left. Junctions and traffic were not for him. He flew across the road and whizzed past us. We ran to follow but he was up on his pedals now, his coat flapping behind him and going like the clappers. We shouted and hooted and jeered but he didn't slow or turn or acknowledge us in any way at all. As we rounded the corner he was already dismounting on the steps of number six.

Miss James stood on the step wearing her fur coat. In her hand she held a sandwich and a cup of tea. 'Glamour Boy' swept off his hat and bowed extravagantly to her. She accepted with a slight nod, then she proffered the snack again. This time he wolfed them down so quickly that he might have taken her fingers off.

Miss James had a head of the whitest hair I had ever seen, moulded to her head almost like a cap. She stepped back and regarded the man on the steps below her. Her stern old face betrayed no sign of emotion. The man was neither welcomed nor turned away. He was simply there and was being dealt with. 'Glamour Boy' finished his snack and gave the plate and cup back to her. He said something to her and she nodded again. He gave a roar of mad laughter that quite shocked us sitting watching from a distance. Miss James was unmoved.

'Glamour Boy' shook his head in disappointment, then mounted his bike and wobbled away out of the terrace to his next appointment. As he passed us he looked at us. He was smiling a lopsided smile. Then he farted loudly. We laughed, but we shivered too at the storm that was going on in his head.

Miss James was going out. Her wooden-framed Bullnose bounced slowly down the drive, heaving in and out of potholes and sending waves of muddy water surging to the kerb. She was vaguely aware of children running after her and slapping the sides of the car but she didn't acknowledge them. Once she was in her beloved car she was in her own sealed little world.

Settled on the worn leather seats she was released from the daily boredom of life with her sisters. In here she could escape from their nagging, fussing and fretful efforts to look after her. Such nonsense, of course. They meant well but she didn't need their ministrations to ease her day.

The Lord was on her side and she had Faith. Sometimes she despaired of the Irish with their ridiculous attachment to Catholicism. It was the colourful trappings they loved not the theology. She could safely say that she'd never met a Catholic who could discuss theology with her. The Bible was a closed book to them. A piece of Protestant luggage, cold and black. She'd long given up worrying about them because for all their faults they were a charming people. She smiled at Culhane who stood and saluted her. A nice man. Tall and straight. Yes they were feckless and lazy, it went without saying, but they were a nice handsome race. She'd always liked people who understood horses. She turned out of the terrace thinking that a spin down to Sandycove would be just the thing for a windy day.

The Avenue was full of strollers, wrapped up against the chilly wind. She progressed down the Avenue at a steady fifteen miles an hour. It was good to be able to get out. Freedom was a most important thing. Too little value put on it these days. She'd never have survived in India without some sense of initiative. It wouldn't have done at all to be useless there.

What sweet children they'd been at the school. And so well disciplined. Eager to learn everything. They wanted to learn and that was the secret. Rows of perfectly charming brown faces and you could hear a pin drop.

Oh, but the heat at midday was intolerable! Perfectly dreadful. One had to lie in the shade and wait for it to cool and hope that a puff of wind might waft through the window. Of course, there weren't enough servants to go around when it came to fanning. People thought they had been very wealthy but they hadn't. Not really. They'd been simple teachers living a quiet life. But it had had its moments of excitement. She smiled as she remembered that fearful cad Jenkins who'd come out from Cardiff, or some such frightful place, to work as an overseer in Assam. A small, burly little man who wore tweeds. Tweeds in that weather! Why he was a laughing stock from the moment he stepped off the boat.

His shirt collar was always stiff and tight and his poor, chubby little face was like a bright cherry under his hat. They used to encounter the wretch at the Home and Empire Club on Saturdays. Edith had been outraged when the man sat down at their table without so much as a by-your-leave.

They'd had to speak sharply to him, very sharply indeed. He'd looked at them, stupefied, as if struggling to understand what they'd said to him. Then he'd jumped up and sent the drinks flying. Why, and then, he'd stepped back to get away from them only to walk straight into a palm plant. Sent the whole thing crashing across the white tiles of the verandah. Even Alim, normally so solemn, had burst out laughing.

She'd never met Jenkins again but they did hear that he had started to drink heavily at work. Later he was fired. Hand in the till, she shouldn't wonder. Oddly enough she always thought of the poor man fondly. She supposed it was because he had provided them with amusement. There now! She'd better buck up. All this thinking and she'd nearly had that man in the gutter. The Bullnosed Morris sailed around the corner towards Dun Laoghaire.

22

He felt a bit of a fool to be standing on the pavement across the road from the office. He didn't want to go in. He was certain of that but there was a part of him that would have loved to have been able to glide through the office, unnoticed by Healy and Hennessy, and nudge Sheridan as he was about to sign an important document.

He moved back off the edge of the pavement and stood by a shop window. He was aware of being conspicuous, standing there at this hour of the day. The others might be looking down on him right now. His watch said quarter past eleven. They wouldn't be coming out for lunch until one or half past. Quite suddenly he felt alone and very miserable.

The office was housed in a run-down building in dire need of a lick of paint around the windows. He pictured the stuffy, badly lit cubby holes inside. It was a horrible place but it was real. People earned their living in there while out here in the street he felt like a fraud and a coward. A coward wasn't too strong really. It took courage to trudge into work day after day. He didn't have it and therefore he'd failed in the one simple mission he'd been set in life. He'd failed to provide. Even the wretched Hennessy was up there now, providing away for his mother down in the country.

He couldn't face them. He'd gloomed himself out of it. Nothing on earth would drag him across the road and in through those familiar doors with their peeling green paint. He would contact Healy again, but in his own time and in his own way. The rest could rot.

He lit a cigarette and looked in the shop window. It was a newsagent's he'd often slipped out to in the past. There was little in the window except a few fading boxes of chocolates and some out of date magazines. He looked up and saw that the shopkeeper was standing at the window looking at him and smiling. He grinned back. The man knew him. He held up his watch and pointed at it. The shopkeeper wagged his finger at him and gave a sly, knowing look. The man's pantomime made him feel uncomfortable but he nodded his head and laughed back. Then he put his finger to his lips and winked. The shopkeeper winked back.

He turned away and walked quickly up the street. The incident irritated him. It was like mitching off from school and being seen by a neighbour. He threw his fag into the gutter, crossed the road and turned right into a long and mean-looking street.

Deliberately he set off up it. He would leave the pretty parts of town until later. He felt a sudden urge to see places he'd never been before, not in all his years working with the others.

The shops and offices were soon left behind. Now there were small, run-down hotels and boarding houses. Men sat out on the steps of some of them. Though it was school time he could see there were plenty of children about.

On his right the buildings gave way to a vacant lot. There were children playing there, a large group of girls and boys. The eldest, about ten or eleven, were running after something. They had stones and were hurling them at their prey. He saw it was a cat. The creature broke into the open and ran towards him. A howl went up and the animal was pursued with a hail of stones. None of them hit it but their raucous screams made him shout at them. They stopped. The cat ran by him and across the road. The children gathered in a sullen group. They stood with stones in each hand clacking them together and watching him. He felt angry but said nothing. The shout had been enough and the cat was gone. He walked on. A stone clattered by him along the pavement. He whirled around and they broke up and ran in several directions, screeching abuse as they went. Bloody gurriers he cursed.

As he walked he noticed there were more and more open windows, more and more people. There was washing hanging everywhere and voices chattering at every door. Every time his eye met another he felt he was under scrutiny. Perhaps they thought he was the landlord or his agent. He looked down at his heavy overcoat. Maybe they thought he was the police. He glanced up. The open windows seemed to be occupied with women taking washing in, putting it out or simply leaning on the sill passing the time with neighbours above and below them.

There were bins dotted all along the street and the air smelt strongly of vegetables rotting. A child darted out of a house and across the road. The boy wore only a vest. A man grabbed him and brought him back to a woman who had now appeared. She wrenched the boy away and hit him hard in the face. The boy grunted. Not satisfied she hit him again. This time he cried. His face was bleeding. She dragged him, screaming now, back into the house.

Father stood, unsure of himself. He'd come too far along the street to turn back. The few side turnings didn't inspire confidence. He decided to head on for the big square he knew was at the top of the street. From there he could easily stroll down to the centre. He bowed his head and hurried on.

Twenty minutes later he was walking at a much more leisurely pace down O'Connell Street. He felt relaxed and comfortable. There were plenty of people about, strollers and shoppers. There were two young Guards standing in the middle of the street. The presence of the two officers re-assured him. They were two solid citizens who exuded a calm authority. A much misunderstood band of men he thought. His eldest son dismissed them as culchies. He felt it was wrong. They were a fine body of men. All that stood between them and anarchy if one were but to think about it for a second. After all his own father had been one.

He walked by them. Children rushed past him shouting and for a moment he thought of that other band of sullen rock-toting brats back in the side streets. God in heaven! What the hell were their parents about, letting them rampage around when they should be at school. He thought of the women washing and the men sitting on the steps. They were frightening people.

His steps took him past cafés and cinemas, the General Post Office and the Pillar. He could feel the pulse of the city here. He crossed to the middle of the broad street and stood by a large statue of a lost leader. He looked up at the offices above the shops. Somewhere up there was probably just the man he wanted to talk to. Somewhere up there, behind those windows in an office there was a publisher. Even now the poor man was struggling through a dreadful manuscript sent to him from Bally-God-Knew-Where.

His eye ran along the nondescript windows and he tried to imagine what a publisher's office might look like. He saw a large desk, covered in sheaves of paper. There was a bookcase against one wall and the gilt lettering of the leather-bound books glittered in the sunlight. On a small table there were a few bottles together with glasses and a pitcher of iced water.

The day would come when he was invited into such an office. The publisher would smile and usher him into a chair. A drink would be offered and accepted. They would talk about Literature. The publisher would say how much he had admired the work on O'Donnell and he would modestly accept the compliment. Then the publisher would unfold plans for a follow-up or even a series. He would smile and reveal that he had had just such a plan in mind.

The publisher would laugh with delight and exclaim how pleasant it was to be talking with a professional writer rather than a dilettante. Father would smile happily and they would clink freshly re-filled glasses. Almost apologetically a contract would be produced and quickly signed. Then Jack would rise, shake hands and make his way back on to the street, a fully fledged member of the city's literati.

Standing there in the street he hugged himself with the pleasure of those thoughts. Such a simple thing really. It wasn't as though he were demanding that much, not in the great scheme of things. He wondered which door he would enter. One with several brass plates caught his eye as a building likely to house a publisher. It occurred to him that it was about time he began to look up the addresses of these people.

His thoughts were disturbed by an abrupt shove from behind. He turned, angry at the interruption. There was a tinker woman at his elbow. She was wrapped in a plain coarse brown shawl and wore a bright red headscarf. Her face was blank and her words dull.

'Can ye spare a few coppers for the childer?' She held out her hand. When he didn't respond she showed the contents of her shawl. He saw then that she carried a baby. The child's face, which was all that showed, was blue with cold and snot trickled from its nose. He wondered if the child was hers. Her blank look hid any expression so that it was hard to tell if she'd ever been pretty. He had an impulse to walk away. His few pennies couldn't help her. Then he remembered his thoughts of just a few moments before. He gave her a sixpence. She started to thank him but he waved her off and set his face towards the river a hundred yards off.

Half way across the road he changed his mind. He had to run back as a car accelerated towards him. The driver was a young man who poked his red face out the window and shouted at him. His passenger, a young girl, laughed back at him from her seat and waved cheekily.

Carefully now he made his way to a pub and stepped into its cool, dark welcome. The noise of the traffic died away as the door swung to. There were only two other customers. The barman had been reading a paper but he looked up as soon as Jack entered and took his order for a pint.

As he took the first bittersweet sip of his Guinness he was suddenly engulfed by a feeling of loss. He would have liked to be part of it all again. How nice it would be to sit here drinking after a day's work with a few friends. To plan, to challenge and to tease with the others. Not now. Too late. They'd not be stirring out for a good few hours yet. Besides he'd no intention of walking all the way back down there just on the off chance that they might go for a few late lunchtime jars.

He looked about him. Both of the other customers were old men, retired from some modest job to judge by their threadbare suits. He felt a twinge of guilt. At least they had a right to be here. He half expected one of them to cross over and present him with a white feather. He swivelled on his stool so that he could keep an eye on the door and the street beyond. Through the glass he could just make out the heads of passers-by. He smiled to himself. Who the hell was he expecting to see here at this hour of the day. This wasn't one of his regular stops and he was sure that none of the others used it.

It was a small, dark little bar with half-partitions of wood along the counter. The sort that leant an air of privacy to the place. There was a lounge upstairs but he'd never used it. Probably the odd couple might pop up there for a drink on their way home. The pub was handy for the bus stops by the bridge.

It surprised him to realize that his pint was nearly drained. There were perfect rings all the way down to the bottom. It pleased him to see it. He nodded to the barman who rose and did the business.

He rooted about in his pockets and checked his money. In all it came to about thirty-five shillings. He pulled out his cigarettes and checked them. There were fifteen. Everything in fives. He liked that. The matchbox was full. He could settle in for a siege here. He was a free agent. His pint was perfect and he marvelled at the consistency of Dublin Guinness. May it always be thus, he thought, as he sipped the head.

23

Outside the dark panels of Father's bar things were changing. The people had grown weary of Devotame. The Soldiers of Destiny had gently shunted him aside and were now led by the bull Lemass. Behind the portals of the party headquarters they had argued like this.

He's old, they'd muttered.

Time to give another fella a crack of the whip.

Not what he was. Not a patch.

Of course we owe him a lot. No one doubts that for a second.

A great man. A truly great man.

But *tempus fugit*, old boy, and the eyes aren't what they were. God knows what he might sign without knowing it.

Elevate the old boy. That was the perfect solution. Make him President of the Republic.

A position of immense dignity and honour.

Just what the old boy deserves after so many years of service.

There isn't a constituency in the land that he hasn't visited at least once.

I bet that's some class of record.

He's stomped the length and breadth of the land for thirty-five years.

Longer.

Longer. And given his very sweat and blood to it.

Time for a rest.

Let someone else take stock of what's been accomplished.

Devotame knew it himself. He felt the strain of having to be in control all the time. His party agreed with him. The burly Lemass could feel power within his grasp. He had his own schemes for the country. By the time he'd finished no one would be laughing at the Irish anymore. The century was more than half gone and he was going to chase down the rest of it.

There would be no peat fires or dancing at the crossroads. Every day Lemass saw that the Dubliners were looking out beyond the Bay for ideas. English fashions, American slang. You couldn't stop them. It was a tidal wave and he didn't intend to go under. He would show the young that he had modern ideas as well. There were plenty to back him.

Time and history had won. Devotame had bowed out and had become President of the Republic. He'd taken up residence in the bucolic surroundings of Phoenix Park from where he emerged from time to time to raise his top hat to visiting heads of state.

Lemass came into his inheritance. He huddled with members of his government, learned professors and clever civil servants. They spent long evenings in debate and incantations for the renewal of Eire were muttered. After months of this they emerged from behind heavy doors with a master plan for economic expansion. A Five-Year Plan no less! Hats were thrown in the air and the clergy advised the people to assist the great venture by working hard and steering clear of industrial strife.

They spread the news. Men stood in bars in Galway and listened, their heads to one side and afterwards they discussed it in low tones over pints. They concluded that it might be a good thing but that only time would tell.

The clubs around Stephen's Green were filled with dark-suited men talking business in corners. They were the new men. They had studied but were not so far from the land that they could be fooled easily.

They sat forward on the edges of comfortable club armchairs holding their whiskys and sodas. They spoke from the side of their mouths as if they thought their rivals might be listening. Really that's exactly what they did want. Then they could enjoy being accused by them of being 'dark horses' and 'fly ones'. That made them feel good, in touch, modern. They would smile modestly and study the toe of a beautifully polished shoe.

'Well, a man's got to make a living, lads,' one would say.

How they would roar with laughter about what a great lad he was. Such a card to describe it as a 'living' and him coining it in. Then he would rise and shout a greeting to an arrival on the far side of the room.

'Sorry, men,' he'd say, edging around them, 'I've just got to see this fella here. Bit of business. Love ye and leave ye.'

The others would watch him go and shake their heads, lost in admiration for his business sense. Then they would discuss their own ventures and each would puff his neighbour up so that in no time at all they were all doing very well for themselves in the ruthless world outside.

They were damned pleased with Lemass. Just the fella to shake the country up. It was about time that things got moving. They were in danger of becoming a laughing stock. Well, Lemass was the fella to show them and the old boys could look out for themselves because there'd be no passengers from now on. Time to cut out the dead wood.

Then they'd all sit back, well pleased with themselves, and order another well-earned round of drinks.

24

It was getting dark outside. Now how the hell had that happened? The barman was shouting and roaring at them to leave him in peace to get some food.

He stood up. He felt just a little tipsy. Not so that an observer would notice, but inside the alcohol pounded him. He pulled on his coat. Good corned beef sandwich here. He must remember that. He drained his glass, picked up his fags and made for the door.

He was the last to leave and, though the barman said goodbye, his arm waved him out impatiently. The two elderly men were still standing outside. They looked as though they intended to spend the Holy hour propped against the wall of the pub. Mentally he downgraded them. Probably worked for the corporation. Once.

He moved off across the road to the bridge feeling the chill wind whip into his face. It was just like the evening he'd left the office for the last time. He stopped on the bridge and looked over the parapet into the water below. Gulls flew between him and the Liffey.

Off down the docks there was a ship moving slowly out into the estuary. It was no more than a grey outline from where he stood. As it reached the middle of the river, a ray of sun hit it, transforming it into an ocean liner bound for Capri.

He sighed. He felt lonely and in a vague sort of way scared. Yes just standing there with everything whirling around him made him shiver.

There were more tinkers on the bridge. They sat, wrapped in shawls, with their hands out. Their younger children dodged in and out of the crowds. Sometimes they singled a person out and followed them all the way across the river, walking backwards, begging. He watched their grimy, wild faces. Their mouths moved in ceaseless beseeching and he wondered it they ever thought about what they said or varied it in any way.

He waited for a group to cross the bridge then ducked in among them. He was past the tinkers and on to the Southside. Rattling his pockets he realized that his needs were as great as theirs. There was less in his pocket than he'd thought.

He gave Fleet Street a glance but didn't linger. It was just another wrong turning and it didn't do to dwell too much on those. Besides there was definitely more prestige in writing than in grinding hackery for that motley shower.

He walked up by the college and stood for a while at a bakery window. Trays of fresh cream cakes and mountains of crusty brown rolls were arrayed in front of him. Already the sandwich seemed inadequate and his stomach rumbled in agreement. He went in and bought a cream slice with strawberry jam on it. The girl gave him a little triangle of cardboard to balance it on.

He walked quickly up to the Green and picked out a bench. The cake deserved nothing less than a seat while it was eaten. He couldn't recall the last time he'd had a cake like this from a shop. The cream really was fresh and he rather suspected that the jam was the genuine article as well.

The scarlet of the jam oozed through the cream and he caught a dollop with his finger and held it for a moment. It really was quite a startling red. Vivid, bloody.

Quite suddenly he saw himself on a railway embankment in Kerry. It was a bright, warm summer's morning. He was in his Captain's uniform, though his Sam Browne was unbuckled and his cap lay on the grass beside him.

Their mission, to repair telegraph lines, had been accomplished and now the men were taking a break before setting off back for barracks. A stream ran along the foot of the embankment and several of the men were sitting beside it, dangling their feet in the water. The others were sprawled about on the grass. Great brown boots lay everywhere along with badly blancoed webbing.

The men were noisy and relaxed. The enemy was all but beaten. They had not been in action for three months now. Even as they frolicked, old Devotame was criss-crossing the hills on horseback trying to persuade the Irregulars to surrender.

He would be glad when it was over. Captaincy, he felt, didn't suit a seventeen-year-old. It was bogus sitting here in his fine uniform with a rank which he'd done nothing to earn. A youth was a youth and the men knew it. He was in command of men twice his age and for no better reason than that he'd been to school. He much preferred dealing with pay from the office but they'd been short staffed.

Away to his left he could see a dipper perched on a rock under a stone bridge. He adjusted his fieldglasses. There was a flash of a white patch on the front. The rest of the body was the kind of brown that looked jet-black in this light. The bird dived into the water, circled the rock and hopped back up on it. In the sunlight he could see its eye winking at him.

He put down the binoculars and took a swig from his canteen. The water tasted warm and he spat it out. He stood up and buckled his belt. 'Come on, men,' he said, 'the sooner we're off the sooner we'll be back in barracks.' He tried to give his voice a rough, manly tone to make the command more acceptable.

Grudgingly, the men rose and began to collect their belongings. Larkin remained seated by the bank. Larkin picked up his rifle and placed the barrel carefully in his mouth. He saw the man's toe wiggle on to the trigger. There was a loud red explosion.

A round, bloodied object rose high above them. Quite slowly, it seemed to him, the gore arced out into the stream and fell with a splash. For a second it was carried downstream, then the top of Larkin's skull sank below the surface.

A loud splash snapped them out of it. Larkin's shattered body had keeled over into the water. They had rushed forward. They'd pulled the man back on to the bank and had puked their guts up when they saw the state of his head.

They'd sent a lorry out from barracks to collect the remains. Questions were asked but no blame was attached to anyone.

Larkin had been 'odd', 'queer', 'quiet'. Must have been some kind of depression. No one could have known. He left no family so that was all right, the authorities said.

He thought he'd left all that behind. It had been years since he'd seen that obscene clay pigeon in his mind and now without warning here it was. He forced his eye away from the oozing jam and took a deep breath, then threw the remainder in a bin. No family. What about us? They hadn't thought about that. Larkin was just a poor demented farm labourer from the bogs. Who knew what had gone on in the man's mind? War did strange things, didn't they say? The doctor had actually said that when he'd heard how the man had killed himself. 'Tut, tut, what a mess!' Then he'd ushered them all out of the temporary morgue. He could remember Larkin's big boots sticking out from under the sheet. They must have been size twelves and they were on the wrong way round.

25

While Father pinted the day away and toyed with anguish, I feel that I ought to point out that there were flaws in his artistic stand. Far from being a wild rebel he was very keen on law and order. He was also a fervent believer in private property. This belief included making me responsible for our railway bridge. Now that winter was behind us, I dreaded the approach of summer.

Every summer the coastline filled with strangers. They roamed and marauded through the landscape, spreading terror among the inhabitants. They swarmed out of the city by train and bus and bicycle. Some merely folded their togs under their arms and walked out.

One whiff of salt on a sunny day and they were transported into an ecstasy. No bridge was too inaccessible, no laneway too forbidding for them as they sought a spot to strip off and plunge their city-white limbs into the cool of the Bay. The carefully painted signs meant nothing to them. They ignored the neatly trimmed lawns. They traipsed, slouched and shambled their way down to the water and they were not to be diverted from their mission.

The terrace was private. Father and the neighbours were inflexible about that. Access to outsiders strictly forbidden. The adults were obsessed by casual passers-by using it as a short cut across 'our' bridge to the sea. We were warned to challenge all interlopers.

At the first sign of decent weather we children took up our positions by the bridge ready to challenge all comers. Every arriving train meant more gurriers. Rough, tough boys. Stone throwers and litterers. They had to be stopped we were told.

Danger was worst in the afternoon when they began to make their way back to the station from every direction. Then they were too tired from a day's swimming and sunbathing to care how they got on to that platform as long as they did.

Picture this. I am sat in a semi-circle with two of my pals. We have just crapped, collectively, on the leafy floor of our camp. We hold our mickies so we won't piss on our sandals and shorts. Round dock leaves are ripped from close at hand to wipe our bums with. We hear footsteps on the metal bridge. We explode from the bushes in howling ambush.

'Hey, you can't cross here, it's private!' I lower my voice to what I hope is a tough gruffness. There are two of them. The younger is about seven, his brother maybe ten. Cheap and torn towels under their arms and a bag of winkles each.

'Why can't we? Jasus, the station's only there.'

''Cause I say you can't, that's why. This place is private. You can go and hop over the wall down there.'

I point to a spot where no conflict will be involved.

'But it's quicker this way.'

'Yeah, but we're not letting ye get over this way cause it's private.'

The pale faces look at one another. The younger one spits.

I sense weakness so I move forward and push one. It lacks conviction.

'Get your fooking hands off me!'

'Go on, move off!' They move some yards down the bridge.

'Go on all the way. Right back on to the rocks.'

'Can't we wait here? We're not doing any harm.'

I'm not sure what to do. My back-up are losing interest. After all they don't live on the damn terrace so why should they care? They stand back watching what I will do.

I rush towards the older boy who takes up a defensive stance. I close with him, briefly, in an awkward waltz, swinging out of each other's sleeves. The others can't hear. I hiss in his ear.

'Listen there's a place to get down on to the platform right behind you.'

At first he seems not to understand. Then he lets go of his grip and backs away. His brother picks up his towel.

124

'Where?'

'Just here.' I show him and they both clamber down. Once down he shouts back.

'You're fooking claimed! I've got a brother and when we come back tomorrow he's gonna kick the shite outta you. Ya cunt!'

I see an adult go indoors on the terrace and I wonder were they watching my performance. I see a pale face hanging out the window of a town-bound train. He is still hurling threats at me. I cannot take my eyes off him. I feel fear and I hate the adults for it.

I only mention my role as guardian of private property because it is so much at odds with the wild Bohemian image that my father would like to have projected. I suppose he wanted an artist's life with a fence around it. Let us go back to the cool bar where he is. He is approached by a stranger.

'I've got twenty-five pounds and a diver's watch.'

'A diver's watch. Really?'

'Absolutely. The real McCoy. That's all I've got left.'

Father studied his pint. The man was loud and drunk. Amiable so far but who could tell where it might lead. He was one of those drunks whose constant demands for attention could turn to violence the second he wasn't given it. Father gave a careful nod.

'Fucking years I was doing the dirty work of this shagging city and all I've got to show for it is this poxy watch.'

The man slammed a large, thick, sturdy watch on the counter. The glass was cracked and one of the hands was missing. Come to think of it Father didn't know if there were supposed to be two hands or not. He supposed it must be two but didn't wish to ask.

There were three or four other men standing around the bar. The spectacle of the local character boring a victim amused them and they laughed maliciously behind their pints and nudged one another.

'Oh, the bodies I've seen!' the drunk lunged forward at him.

'Easy now, Tony,' said the barman, 'that's enough of that.'

'Oh right you are, John, right you are so,' Tony lowered

his voice and hissed at him. He wished the man would find someone else but he was tired and drunk and besides Tony was determined to have his audience.

'Bodies swollen up like balloons. Purple and green. Oh, every colour of the rainbow so they were. The worst were the ones in the cars with their faces all twisted up and their fingers curled, scraping at the windows trying to get out.'

Father tried to attract the others and muttered, 'Terrible, Terrible.' None of them accepted his offer to join the conversation. Tony whirled around and glared at them.

'What are you looking at? Do you want a dig or what?'

The others stepped back and shook their heads. Father made a move to slip off his stool but the man rounded on him.

'Took me hours to get them out. Hours. Up and down I was. Sick as a dog for days afterwards. Oh yeah. Hard stuff. Hard stuff that. They called me a hero then. The papers had it. Tony Brown – hero. I was too. I fucking was a hero!'

'Ah sure you still are, Tony,' one of the others called.

'I fucking know I am, but does this man here?'

Oh shit, Father thought, he's talking to me. Just go away and leave me alone. For Christ's sake, did this gobhawk not know that he was ruining things with his shouting and his violence?

'Well, you sound like a hero and who'd deny you?' That sounded right he hoped.

'Well, buy us a drink then, for fuck's sake! I'm not after telling you me life story for nothing now, am'nt I? Am'nt I? A pint, for Jasus sake!'

Father called the barman over and ordered a pint for the ex-Port diver.

'That's no use! No use at all. Are you not having a drink too?'

'Ah no, I'm all right. I've got to be heading off as a matter of fact. Got to get a bus out. Last train's gone.'

Father rose and began to leave. His size threw the drunk for a moment and Father started for the door. He didn't move quickly enough for the drunk lurched at him and grabbed his wrist.

'Come outta that! Don't be such a miserable bollocks!'

Father felt his face flush. He knew there was a forced smile on his face. The pub seemed full of grinning men all looking at him. Some were laughing, others were merely puzzled. Men stood up from their tables to get a better look at what was going on. He tried to pull away again. There were others closing in behind him blocking his passage to the door. The barman had disappeared to the cellar. The drunk was appealing to his audience now. His free hand was flapping about. He was like a mad barker with a circus bear.

'This snobby shite won't have a drink with me! Can ye beat that, lads? He won't have a drink with Tony Brown. Thirty years a diver in the Port. A hero. A bloody hero and this fella won't have a drink with me!'

Father gestured vaguely at the pint he'd just bought the man and tried to look helpless.

'All very well, but you haven't got one yerself. Can't be bothered to sit and drink with me? Well I'm not some bloody tinker that you can buy off with a drink. I'm a diver. A qualified diver.'

The barman suddenly emerged from a hatch in the floor. Wiping his hands on his white apron, he took in the spectacle. 'Ah, for Jasus sake, lads, break it up or ye'll have the Guards in on top of us. Tony leave go of that man now, there's a good man.'

The grip on his sleeve slackened and Father tore his arm away.

'Sorry about that, sir,' said the barman.

The spell was broken. The drunk turned away, shrunken and powerless. People began talking and Father heard the clink of glasses. Where there had been a wall of men barring his path a moment before, there was now only one old man sipping at a bottle.

Ignoring the barman's 'goodnight' Father plunged out the door into the street. As the doors swung to behind him he heard a great guffaw of laughter and was sure that he could hear the barman and the drunk among them.

He rushed away down the streets. His head was spinning and he was hungry. A nice big slice of corned beef with some spuds would be just the thing. The thought made him hungrier but there was little in his pockets now. All about him the shops were closed and dark. The few people about walked by hurriedly, huddled against the cold, stinging rain which now fell in sheets.

He pulled his hat down and did his coat up. Then walked to the corner and stood, undecided. He had only a few shillings left and he had drifted away from his usual haunts. Healy and the others would be long gone by now.

As he stood there, swaying, a car passed at speed and sent up a huge wave of water. Awkwardly, he jumped back to avoid the spray and fell, heavily, over some dustbins. Reaching out to lever himself upright, his hand clasped something sharp and jagged making him gasp. The pain was intense. He scrabbled to his feet and stumbled to a streetlight.

He held up his hand. There was a gash and blood flowed freely from the wound. It dripped down his sleeve and ran off his fingers on to the wet pavement. He found his handkerchief and pressed it against the cut. It turned crimson.

This wasn't what he'd imagined his day would be like at all. It wasn't right that it should end like this. He'd just come in for a few drinks and a mooch around. Well, bugger it, anyway! Shag that gobshite in the pub! Shag the whole fecking lot of them! He didn't have to put up with this. He had a home to go to. Where was the bus stop now? Where the hell was this? For a while he couldn't remember exactly where he was. He knew the street all right but he couldn't place where it led to.

His knee began to ache. He looked down and saw that there was a rip in his trousers. He felt inside and his fingers came away damp with blood.

'Ah, for sweet Jasus sakes! What's going on here. I'm destroyed!'

A dog howled far away, its voice carrying in the night. He saw the lights of a bus and made for the spot. Walking was difficult but he began to recognize where he was.

'Oh, gameball. We're all right now. No problem. Just down here and turn right and I should . . . eh . . . should, that's the one! Knew I was right. Soon be on a bus out of this hole.'

When the bus lurched around the corner he hauled himself on board and sagged into a downstairs seat. When he'd settled he noticed the other passengers looking at him. He took off his hat and ran his fingers through his hair. His reflection in the window shocked him. He hardly recognized the dishevelled wreck looking back at him. There was blood on his face. He must have rubbed his torn hand there. The cut on his hand had a ragged edge to it and the skin had turned white.

The conductor came and took his fare. Father ignored his questioning look and stared out of the window. The bus followed the line of the Bay home. Father sat staring out at a spring day turned to wintery evening because this was Dublin. As he sat he thought of Larkin's shattered skull sailing so slowly down into the water.

26

The news from the country was not good. Her father was dying. Ellen knew what that meant. She would have to bring Grandma up from Killarney to live out her days with us. Mother said that she wished she could find it in herself to welcome her mother but it just seemed so unfair.

An out of season holiday was quickly arranged and we younger ones were bundled aboard a south-bound train. Mother didn't trust the others to feed us. Lunch was the problem. We went to the little terraced house where Grandma lived and where Mother had been brought up.

We passed the time playing with gangs of kids who never seemed to be at school. We were taken on outings on jaunting cars. Mother knew all the jarvies personally it seemed. Once or twice I had lingered nearby as she negotiated with them. She paid no attention to the prices they had up on their boards. Rather she waded in with her own itinerary and defied them with a brand of logic that they were unable to follow. If they resented her, it never showed. Once the bargain was struck the leather-faced drivers were happy to do it her way and let us drive as well.

Grandmother seemed very quiet when we got back from these jaunts. She would be sitting by the table, waiting for us in the gloom. She would smile and we'd run to her as always but now she spoke over our heads to Mother.

'No change today' it would be or, 'He's weaker. It can't be long now.'

We knew what they were talking about but we hadn't seen him for a very long time and I could only recall a loud and angry man who kept a roaring fire, even in summer.

At night they would shoo us out and then sit together in a vigil and make tea for the occasional neighbour who dropped in for a hushed chat. Mother said that Uncle Gerald, down the terrace, would be pleased to see us.

The old man sat deep in a battered armchair. The covers had split at the arms and the rough, black horsehair stuck out in tufts. His arse rested on an old blanket because the leather seat of the armchair had long since given up the unequal struggle and had burst asunder. Uncle Gerald recalled that he'd bought the chair from a man in Glin for two shillings, thirty years before.

In that chair he'd done all his thinking and had taken most of his major decisions. In it he'd decided not to get married, though he knew the woman would have had him like a shot. He'd sat and stared at the smouldering peat for most of a whisky night and then had decided against it. He was perfectly capable of looking after himself and he kept a better house than most.

All his bits and pieces had their place and he knew just where to put his hand on anything he wanted. His tobacco tin sat on a stool to his left and the old copper kettle sat in the hearth. His specs hung on a nail, handily hammered into the wall by the fireplace. His table and chairs stood in the middle of the room and, if they weren't brand new, there was plenty of wear in them. A pine dresser stood against the wall and he had cups and crockery enough to have six people in to sit and eat. Davey and I loved the smell of it and squatted by the fire.

In his chair he had decided that most of his neighbours were not much to write home about when it came to passing the time of day or having a bit of crack in the pub. They were a miserable crew who had no time for time. Having made up his mind that they were a collection of gobdaws, he ignored them.

There were exceptions. People like Glenny Mac. Sound man, Glenny. As good a pal as a fella could hope for. Many's an evening they'd supported one another, swaying and staggering their way from Johnny O's. Johnny was a decent skin himself.

131

'Tough old birds, all of us,' he grunted, as we hunkered down by the fire. He seemed quite happy for us to be there. He asked after Mother and Grandmother and made sounds that might have been sympathy but could just as easily been him clearing his throat.

'How do you think I survived a place like Chicago?'

A younger Gerald had been driven out of the country by the lack of land and prospects and had sailed away to Amerikay. Once there he had made straight for Sheecago where he knew there were plenty of Munstermen to be found. He had no difficulty in finding digs with a Mrs Farrell whose parents still lived in Dingle.

'Straight into the police and no mistake,' he told us. 'Ah sure, there wasn't a gangster in the whole of Chicago that I didn't know. It was great gas back in them days and no messing.'

He paused there for a while to get the order of things right in his head and gave the smoky peat fire a poke with a crooked poker. Everything smelt of peat and the tiny fireplace was stained brown by the smoke.

'The West Side O'Donnells had the lot of them beat and that was the size of it. Sure they were only put on the run when the wops got the big politicians on their side. Capone would never have got the better of the West Side boys without a wink from the mayor and his pals.'

Davey asked what wops were but Gerald seemed not to hear.

'And Dion O'Bannion? Now there was a grand big man with the manners of a prince. A fine big handsome man and polite too. Always a word for us on patrol and a little something for the Christmas box. "Just for the kids, O'Malley," he'd boom out right there on the door of his flowershop. He always had a beautiful rose in his buttonhole.'

Uncle Gerald sighed at the memory. 'I remember the day we were called down there to find him dead. Stone dead, sprawled in a heap on the floor of his shop. Red as the roses he sold. Shot down like a dog. That was Capone for ye! A damn fecking coward him and his crew! Sorry about the language, boys, but there you are.'

He shifted his great gnarled toecap and kicked a piece of peat back on to the fire. I loved listening and kept very quiet, afraid he might stop.

'That's when it all went wrong, you know. When those blasted Eyeties moved in. Ruined the whole damn show so they did! They wanted everything for themselves, the hounds! Ah, I'd no time for them. They lived like pigs and acted like rats. To shoot poor old Dion like that and they held his hand as though to shake it. Can ye credit that for swinery? Dion was a rough houser true enough. But only against his own kind. Never outsiders. Those Capone fellas never gave a tinker's curse who they shot. Great days all the same and no mistake. Hardly a day went by when we weren't called off to do battle. Shot some of them too. Others ended up in the electric chair.'

'Did you see anyone in that?'

'Indeed I did not. *ZZZZZZZZZzzzt*! Just like bacon on that griddle there. You could hear them scream half way down the river. We could do with that for some of them fellas above in the Dail.'

We laughed at this.

'Of course most of them were just guilty of breaking a stupid bloody law. Imagine it! No drink! Quare kind of place that makes it a crime to have a pint, eh? No wonder the lads wanted to smuggle it in. Mr Killjoy Volstead. Some class of a Dutch Prod, I believe.'

I tried to imagine a whole country without drink.

'Dion had the biggest funeral in the States next to Valentino, ye know. Twenty thousand turned out. Hundreds of cars. They used up every flower in his shop and plenty more besides. Every bigshot in town was there. Archbishops too. The Knights weren't afraid to turn up. See Dion was seen as a fine Irishman by a hell of a lot of people. He was too. Every bit as good as some who claimed to be respectable.'

He lapsed into silence and we all sat there, thinking of Dion O'Bannion. I couldn't imagine why they should kill a man who owned a flowershop. I was distracted by the smell of piss in a potty somewhere.

'Generous. I said that but they were too. Money meant nothing to them and they didn't do much harm with it either. The O'Donnells, Tuohy and Moran, all Irish fellas. I knew them and I arrested some of them when they got too far out of line. But they were cool as a breeze about it. In no time at all they'd have a shyster lawyer in there and they'd all be back in the street. We decided that if a phone call was that important to them then we'd ask for a donation to police funds every time they made one. They were delighted to oblige and we made a fair few bob out of it too. Then the Etalians came and people started getting hurt.'

We sat forward, eager for mayhem.

'There was a time when it wasn't safe to go out on the street. Not safe in the street! Can ye picture that?'

I had an image of a West Side O'Donnell wielding his broadsword on a street corner.

'It was like a battlefield at times. You'd come along on a Monday morning and be sure to find a body in the street, face down in the gutter. I've seen some sights, boys, but a man who's been in the river for a couple of months takes some beating. You wouldn't want to have had breakfast that morning I can tell you! God there's be half the face eaten away by fish. *Grrrrch*! Horibble man, horrible! The rest of him would be swollen up like a balloon with the clothes all tight around him. Sometimes they'd burst and my God in heaven, the smell that hit you was one I'll never forget. It's with me now. Still there in the nose.'

I wondered was it like beery piss.

'Taken for a ride, as they'd say in the Windy City. Taken for a ride. Poor Mrs Farrell would put out a big spread for us after the night shift. Sausages, ham, hash browns, eggs. A feed, man. Of course she'd no idea what we'd seen. There were plenty of times when breakfast was the last thing on my mind. But you couldn't offend her so we'd all tuck in. Later, when she'd gone shopping, we'd take it in turns to slip into the bathroom and throw up the lot. The whole blinking lot! It's no wonder we were always ravenous when we went back on the night shift. Oh, she didn't know the half of it and that's for sure.'

Mother bustled in and whispered to Gerald. Then she ushered us back to Grandmother's. The old man lying above in the county hospital was dead.

27

We had a rich and fruitful garden bounded by walls whose cement had long since crumbled to dust from the continual sea spray. They were really dry stone walls. Fruits and flowers grew in colourful profusion and the summers seeped away there like the water in the little pool that Father had made.

The garden was ripe with purple loganberries, orange pippin and swollen Worcesterberries. There were glorious blue lobelia, red roses and banks of marigold. By July it was ablaze.

Its colour and warmth and secrecy attracted Grandmother. She would move a comfy chair from the kitchen and sit in the sunshine. She would settle with an *Independent* over her head. It didn't do to allow the sun on the head. Addling would be sure to result. It wouldn't do, at her age, to be caught in a suntrap. She'd known lads in Listowal go funny from the sun and her own mother had been quick to cover her head whenever the temperatures soared.

Under the paper she could allow her mind to go where it pleased. Often as not it was a strange journey to begin with, full of weird faces and surprises. Faces swam up out of the mist at her and peered into her face. They always went away and she didn't fear them.

Curiosity got the better of her and she began to stare back. One face turned out to be Dinny, a lump of a bully from childhood, whom she'd never been afraid of. Another was her brother Jim, smiling crookedly in that way he had. She began to look forward to seeing the different faces and trying to name them.

As the heat took hold she drifted away further and imagined the garden as a slice of the country she'd come from.

A sad day that, packed on to a train with daughter and grandsons and hauled away. Away from Killarney and all she knew, like a shrivelled old crow in widow's weeds. She'd felt numb the whole way and the constant lurching of the train had made her feel sick. Ellen had tried to reassure her by saying that they'd all go back on holiday but she knew that was nonsense.

So she did what she always did to the nice things. She fixed it on her memory and let it settle there. She'd have what she left of her past life, clear as a photo. The funny thing was that now she remembered the cottage with a thatch on it and that had been replaced twenty years earlier with an ugly corrugated iron one which she hated.

As the train had rattled and lurched along she tried to take her mind off the past and imagine how the city might have changed. This wasn't her first time and the memories flooded back.

Townsend Street. That's where her dear-departed had fetched up with her in tow, thirty years ago. 'Come on, girl,' he'd said one afternoon, flushed with excitement and beer, 'Dublin's the place. The very place.'

There was nothing she could do, of course. Not when he'd got himself worked up into this sort of mood. He was determined to be gone out of it as soon as possible. Fit to be tied half the time, what with one plan or another. She never questioned his schemes just the half-cocked execution of them. He had a way with him.

How could she resist him after he'd gone and fought for his country's freedom? She shuddered as she remembered the night the Tans had come for him and had hauled him off to Limerick Jail. They'd come in a Crossley tender, bumping and jolting down the unpaved street. Baking bread, that's what she'd been doing at the time, when she looked up and saw them coming up the path. Four of them. Big, strong men with heavy boots and ugly rifles. He'd seen them too.

'Let them in,' he'd said, and she smiled at the memory of his calm face. She whisked the door open just as one of them raised his rifle to hammer on it and the fella had fallen over himself, spilling in through the door. Well, the eff words out of him!

'Where's O'Malley?' they'd shouted, as they peered around them and kicked over chairs just for the racket of it. Then himself had come down to the foot of the stairs, not a hair out of place, wearing a clean white shirt and freshly shaven.

'Here I am,' he'd said, 'shall we go along now?' And he'd walked out the door past them as though he was leading them to their own truck. It was all the neighbours could do to stop themselves from letting out a great roar. She'd been proud of him.

They'd stuck him into jail for six long months and she'd made the journey over to visit him every week. He always had a smile and a laugh for her but jail changed him in some mysterious way. He was edgy and fidgeted. He became agitated and whispered across the partition to her. Once the war was over, he'd said, there's going to be plenty of scope. On and on he'd gone about scope, plenty of scope.

Then he'd been released and the war had run its course only to be followed by another that left the country bitter and twisted with ruined souls. He had lost but he said little. After all there was always scope.

So they'd drifted up from the south, slow and easy. There was hardly a village they passed through where he wasn't taken by some money-spinning notion. He'd work each area for a few days absolutely convinced that there was a fortune to be made there. Then the day would always come when he'd end up back in their poor digs, with his face slapping off his knees with the misery of it all.

'There's no point in carrying on in this place,' he'd groan, as he fell into a chair, 'the locals have the place sewn up and there's no place for a Kerryman. A monopoly is what the bowsies are running here! Dublin, old girl. That's the place. A place to stretch yourself and not feel hemmed in all the time. In a place that size sure there's every chance that a bright spark like myself would get under way in no time at all and not be bothered at every turn by the local crowd.'

28

That summer there were days when the clouds would gather over the Bay like a purple shroud and it would go very still. The sea would stretch out and flatten and we would gather at the end of the bridge and wait for the storm. 'Out of the water!' would go the cry and bathers would sweep up their clothes and towels and sprint for shelter.

Lightning was the fear some said. Others knew that the real reason for this exodus from the sea was that the water turned a very sinister shade of deepest blue when there was a storm in the offing. You never could be absolutely sure what might be swimming below you. Scientists didn't know everything.

Gasps and 'Oohs' would greet the first great flash of lightning over the Pigeon House and the crack of thunder that followed. The clouds would roll over us and lose their colour as they released their torrents.

My friends and I would sit in the porch and wait for it to stop. Comics would be produced and mulled over. Some were swopped, others lent. Gerry had an uncle in America and he would make us all jealous by reading ads for air rifles and War of Independence soldiers. They could be had for dollar cheques and the addresses featured words like Zip Code and Zone.

Gerry said that didn't matter because he would order them direct from his uncle in Buffalo. We forgot to ask him about them when they failed to appear. Usually the rain would stop and play would resume.

There were some evenings when we were stunned by the beauty of the sunset over the city to the north. We would stop our playing and lie on the lawns. The steps and benches would fill up as adults filled the front of the terrace. Not even the

139

clouds of midges under the elm trees bothered us. We would take up our positions near the adults as they talked and swopped opinions. I would stare at the city and try to imagine what was going on there.

I saw elegant avenues down which my sisters strolled with their friends and lovers. Dinner dances in hotels. Women in evening dresses being ushered into waiting taxis. Sometimes – oh, the romance of it! – there would be a horse-drawn cab waiting for the young lovers, to trot them gently around St Stephen's Green before he walked her to the number eleven bus for Terenure.

The impossibly rich visited Jamet's restaurant where ancient waiters served them. The price of a meal in there could feed a family for a fortnight Liam had said. A bit of a Trinity crowd though. Prods in town for the night from Monkstown, or up from Meath for the Spring Show.

I read my sisters' magazines often enough to imagine Dublin as an Irish Cannes when the sun shone. Between those glossy pages everything was just so and all the fit, tanned men carried dashing trenchcoats over their arms. Prince Rainier turned Grace Kelly into a princess and we all feasted on the pictures.

Anne and Mary talked almost daily of going to France and becoming au pairs. Everyone was doing it on the Southside and really it was the only thing for a girl to do.

While they argued about how best to bring their plan to fruition, planes were landing, full of dark Concepcións and Asunciós from Madrid, determined to learn English in Catholic Ireland. On the Northside of town, streets of Conceptas got on with the ironing.

Somewhere a radio played. 'If you must sing a song do sing an Irish song! This programme has been brought to you by Walton's, makers of musical instruments and publishers of sheet music.' Any day was Urney day but Saturday was Lemon's day.

After the storms of spring the Bay had settled down, lulled, perhaps, by an unusually hot spell of weather. On one such day, across a flat, calm sea, a yacht approached, sailing straight and true for the shore where we lay, burning, on our towels.

Coming too close it ran aground, thirty yards from the shore. We surged into the water to get a closer look. Unable to contain myself, I swam in my fastest Pearl Diver stroke, splashing madly.

From below decks there emerged a man. His short blond hair was complemented by a moustache. He wore a khaki shirt and shorts and in his hand he held a drink. I put him in his thirties but it was only a rough guess, adults being of a muchness to me.

He stood there and raised his glass in greeting, first to me and then to all the others in the water and on the shore. He bowed slightly. His skin was deeply tanned and the hair on his legs seemed almost yellow. Behind him a woman came on deck. She was his twin but slim where he was stocky.

I swam a few extra strokes. Their boat was called *The Sea Sprite* and the decking was of a dark mahogany-coloured wood. The rail was brass and at the back it flew a yellow ensign.

The man motioned me to the ladder. When I reached it, he motioned me to stop. I was not going to be allowed on board.

'Good afternoon little man,' he said, in what I thought was a German accent. The woman smiled down at me as I stood waist-deep in the shallows. She said something to him in German and giggled. The man didn't answer her but smiled to himself. He drank his drink and put down his glass.

'It appears that we have miscalculated.' He seemed to think this very funny. He shook his head as he looked at how close to shore he was. 'Yes. A miscalculation. Without doubt we have made a mistake I think. This is not where we want to be. Not at all.' Then he seemed to remember me standing there on tiptoe, straining to look over the side into their boat.

He rummaged in his pockets and produced a ten shilling note.

'Now, my friend. How would you and your friends like to spend this on whatever you damn well like?'

I replied that me and my friends would be delighted to spend ten shillings on whatever we damn well liked and what did he want doing?

'I want you and your friends to push us out of this damn sand. If you can manage this I – and my wife, of course, my wife Bettina here – will be very grateful.'

Try as we might we failed to budge the German's yacht. For a full fifteen minutes we shoved and heaved and pushed and pulled without success. The job was not helped, I felt, by the German's unwillingness to leave the ship. He and his wife sat there with fresh drinks and watched our efforts. Occasionally he would shout encouragement but otherwise they seemed to be engaged in a quiet chat.

'It won't go. Not a chance. Won't budge an inch,' I reported breathlessly to my employer. He seemed to consider this for a minute. Then he shrugged and climbed down the ladder. The woman followed him.

'In that case, my friend, you had better lead us to the shore. We will wait for the tide to do what you and your friends cannot.'

The two Germans were led up across the bridge to the lawns. The adults surrounded them in a friendly horde. Father was there, making a fuss of welcoming them. A table and chairs were brought out though everyone had been happy to sit on rugs before. Mr Sheehan appeared with a couple of bottles and despite glares from Mother poured the two guests a drink. We found ourselves being squeezed to the edge so we settled on the grass and tried to listen. Liam tried a phrase of German on them and they beamed. Encouraged, he continued. This time they looked a little confused. The man listened closely.

'We are very happy with hydroelectricity on the Rhine. It is very good.' He was grinning. 'The last time we looked, ja, it was working fine for sure.'

Everyone laughed. Liam flushed a little. 'Just a thought,' he mumbled and he fixed his eyes on some far off object out by the harbour.

The man introduced himself and his wife. He was Max Rundstedt. There was a Von in his name but he seldom used it. He added that he was not related to the General of the same name. The adults were a little disappointed about that. Max introduced his wife Bettina. They were from Cologne and were on a month's holiday.

142

'Isn't it the grand time of it ye have and no mistake,' Mother said, lighting another Sweet Afton. 'You must be doing something quite high up to be over for that long.'

Mother had no hesitation in asking these sort of questions of total strangers. She saw no reason not to find out as much as possible about them before they sailed off. The other adults gasped at her impertinence and Miss ffrench tutted. But Max wasn't at all put out and answered Mother quite happily.

'Oh, my wife and I can take as much time as we like. Money is not a problem for us.' He waved his hand in a vague way, searching for the right word. 'Washing machines. Yes? That is how you call them? Yes. Washing machines, that is what my factory in Germany makes.'

'We could do with them here,' said my Aunt, 'I'm never done washing duds!'

Everyone laughed except the Germans, who looked puzzled. I felt quite cheated. Washing machines weren't quite what I'd expected from a sun-tanned German yachtsman called Rundstedt.

They all filled their glasses and Father proposed a toast to the guests. Everyone drank happily. Neighbours joined them on the lawn and the talk went on all afternoon.

The tide came in and raised the trapped yacht. The two Germans rose and made elaborate departures. The woman whispered to Max and he looked at me. He came over, grinning: 'Here we are, my friend. For you and your friends. You think I forget.' He handed me the ten shilling note.

Everyone crossed the bridge to watch them get back on their yacht. In the late afternoon sun the tide had crept back in and the yacht now bobbed in deeper water. While we watched, our two visitors shook hands for the last time and then they waded fully clothed into the water and swam at a leisurely pace back out to their vessel.

'A countess. Can ye beat that,' my father said. I latched on to the word and demanded to know. Bettina who'd sat quietly with Max all afternoon turned out not to be German despite appearances, but an Italian from Tuscany and a countess into the bargain.

As their yacht moved past the rocks and out into the Bay I wanted to call them back. I wanted to make them stay and talk about nobility, not washing machines. I had missed her quiet revelation and now it was too late. *The Sea Sprite* was taking them out of our lives.

Later we feasted on vanilla wafers, cream soda, chocolate and toffees. Each bite sought out a new cavity and left deposits there nestling in the black holes, but I was oblivious to the risks. My mind was imagining life on *The Sea Sprite* and how you got to be a crewman for such wonderful people.

29

That summer Father moved his table out on to the front steps every afternoon. There he would sit with his books piled up in front of him and a pen in his hand. He had three large writing pads. Only one had anything written in it but that didn't matter, he had his notes. There in a separate pile were the fruits of all those hours spent in the winter gloom of the drawing room.

He was doing well now he felt. He had a grip again on the elusive northern hero. O'Donnell was clear to him now. The Gaelic chieftain had stepped out of the murky past and stood visible in his mind's eye. It was vital that he get it all down on paper before it faded again.

So he sat there bent over his pad, scribbling furiously, not pausing even to look up at passing neighbours who greeted him from time to time. His forehead gleamed in the hot sun and he felt sweat on his neck but still he wrote on and on. Afraid now to rise and put it away for the day, he no longer knew or cared what his family were doing. Nothing mattered but getting down the outline. The flesh could come later.

His pages were filled with incident and portraits from the sixteenth century. Historians would read this and wonder that a man could bring a bygone age so alive to the reader. There was so much, all in a surge, that he wasn't sure if he could control it.

During his few breaks from the labour he perused his drawings. Now that he saw them in the bright summer light, he wasn't at all sure that they were suitable. The lines weren't as clear as he'd hoped. Some of them were quite childish. He decided that only four out of the ten were any good at all.

Sometimes he would find Ellen placing a cup of tea and a sandwich beside him. He felt hugely grateful and would beam in response. She ignored him. Things were getting better, he felt, but it would take time. Still, if he got this off the ground and it started to sell . . . She'd change her tune when a real publisher turned up.

The thought made him think of that awful day in the city. He would never go in again. Not like that anyway. Slinking around the streets, going to strange pubs, acting as though he didn't care where he drank.

Fortunately they'd all been asleep when he'd stumbled in the back door. He'd stuck his fingers down his throat and thrown up behind the box hedge at the end of the garden. That way no one would hear him going up and down stairs at night. Once inside, he'd stripped off and inspected the damage. He'd bandaged the cut hand and put a cold compress on his knee which was quite blue-looking.

Later he'd found a blanket in the hotpress and had slunk off to the front room and slept the night on the sofa. The next day he explained his presence there by saying that there had been a chapter he'd had to finish. He didn't think they'd entirely swallowed his tale.

His pounding skull took ample revenge for his lies and he could do no work at all for two days. He would never go to town like that again he swore. Next time would be for an appointment and nothing else.

Tom Whelan and Bill Moriarty had called by the day before and he'd sat with them on the steps for a couple of hours. They sat admiring the view while he told them about Max and the Italian countess. When he'd finished he could see that they'd been impressed.

'Having the sea spread out in front of you like this must be a great bonus,' said Bill enviously. 'Sure you'd never know what class of mystery was going to end up on your doorstep. It must be a great source of inspiration for you. Now that you're doing the writing yourself like.'

'Oh, it's a great thing and no mistake,' Tom added. Tom Whelan's house also stood on the edge of the Bay. 'So how's the great work coming along if I may be so bold as to ask?'

It delighted him to be able to tell them that the novel was close to completion. He patted the pile of paper on the table. It felt thick and professional. This wasn't the product of bar room chatter. He could quite easily imagine the comforting pile nestling happily between hard covers. Vaguely he wondered what the publisher's would charge. He hoped it wouldn't be too much. After all he wanted as many punters as possible to read it. The word punter felt a bit silly, even as he thought it. He had thought for a second that a professional writer should view his work with the detachment of a bookie. It didn't work though. Even as he mouthed the word 'punter' it felt false and contrived.

'Oh, there's a deal of money to be made in writing,' Bill said, squinting his eyes against the sun. 'For the fellow who has the right connections that is.' 'You're right there, absolutely right.' Tom agreed, almost shouting. 'It's knowing someone on the inside is the secret.'

He felt good sitting there with them in the sun. Although they irritated him sometimes with their small talk, Bill in particular was almost as obsessed with trespassers as he was himself, the two men at least lent him verbal support and never sneered at his efforts.

He was relieved all the same when they had left. Interruptions and the chance to sit and talk about art would be welcome but only after he had finished the job in hand.

He carried on writing for another half an hour but the noise of children screaming and roaring at play distracted him. He finished a sentence and decided that would be enough for the day. The sun had moved low in the sky and was beginning to dazzle him. He put down his pen and sat back.

He noticed Sheehan had emerged. He hadn't seen his neighbour for weeks now. In fact the entire tribe seemed to have hibernated. Mr Sheehan had crossed to the edge of the lawns above the station. He was carrying a bag. Stopping at the edge he began to take out liquor bottles and throw them down the bank.

There was a crash of glass and a scream of pain. He rushed to the edge of the bank. Sheehan stood there with his finger to his mouth and a sheepish expression on his face.

'What kind of fecking stupid carry on do you call that?' he yelled. Sheehan said nothing. The gobshite just stood there and pointed. A blood-stained face was scrabbling up the bank towards them.

'Jesus Christ, son, what has he done to ye? Has he killed you or what?' Anger at Sheehan's trampish stupidity surged through him. He was almost as surprised as his neighbour when he punched him in the mouth. Then he swept his bloodied son off to hospital for stitches.

I was the bloodied son. Sheehan's bottle had broken on the back of my head and split it open. Cork dry gin I think it was. My presence in the bushes was not because I was taking part in some boyish game of soldiers, but because the bushes were close to the railway bridge. They provided a good vantage point from where to look up the skirts of passing women. It was while doing this that everything went black for a moment or two.

My wound needed several stitches, none of which I accepted gratefully. The nurse seemed quite relieved to see me leave and I arrived home to be cosseted and waited upon. Apart from some pain, my only regret was that it hadn't happened during school term time.

I gathered, from my sickbed, that Sheehan had had a tooth loosened in the exchange with Father but he was not planning to do anything about it. Fear of a massive counter-suit for my injuries ensured that Father didn't have any unpleasant consequences to deal with.

Mother was delighted. It confirmed everything she'd suspected about the Sheehans. They were not just drunks but dirty, tinkerish drunks who behaved abominably without a single thought for innocent children.

Father came and sat on the end of my bed. I sensed he was quite pleased with his handling of the situation because, though he didn't refer to it directly, he continually rubbed his fists together as though he was ready for another fight. Sheehan had become 'the drunken bowsie' or 'the boyo beyond' or 'the bloody smuggler'.

He and Mother seemed to patch things up. My wound acted as a sort of negotiating ploy. They spoke to one another in a way that wasn't exactly affectionate but was friendly enough in tone for me to think that things were back to normal.

My Aunt plied me with a constant supply of oranges and comics. When I grew tired of comics I would lie alone at the top of the house and listen. On windy days the stairs groaned and sighed as the wind whistled in through broken panes on the landings.

On quiet days there was the constant drumming of pigeon wings as they flew in and out of the Sheehans' wrecked roof, the males cooing and billing in an endless puffed-up display of courtship for the scrawnier females.

Other times I would listen for human sounds. I would hear Father rumbling along the hall to his day's work on the great book. He did a good deal of moving around I noticed. No sooner would the front room door close than it would open again and I would hear him huff his way down to the kitchen. He made quite a lot of noise. It seemed to cost him effort and I worried briefly about his health.

Mother would ascend the stairs to turn down beds. On the top landing, just below my room, she would pause and I could hear her muttering incantations against the Sheehans. I crept out to look once. She was standing at the window, right to one side with her face flat against the glass so that she could squeeze as much of the Sheehan house into her view as possible.

Her twisted face appeared quite deranged and her lips moved in a ceaseless tirade of silent curses at her enemy. By the time she'd pulled herself away and come up to my room her temper was often at its worst.

'Damn bloody woman! Doesn't give a tinker's curse about anyone! Selfish bloody so-and-so! Why don't you get up and go out for some fresh air? Nothing will do you but to lie there and waste the whole of the best summer we've had for years. You're under my feet the whole live long day. It would persecute a saint the life I lead!'

Without waiting for my reaction she would shuffle off back down the stairs. My presence in the room spoilt her opportunity to spy because the room gave the best view of the Sheehans and their garden.

There was another sound that I began to notice. At first I thought it came from below me. It was the sound of pipes. Pipes where there had been none before. I got out of bed. As I went down the stairs the sound increased. As it did, it's resemblance to pipes became less obvious. There was metal in the sound but also something drum-like and pounding. Quite suddenly there was a crash as though something had been dropped from a height. This would happen at regular intervals until the sound would die away completely. But the next day it would be back again and each time I heard it I thought I detected a note of increased suffering and stress in the distant rumblings. What there was no doubt about was that the strange sounds came from the Sheehans.

30

I took Mother's advice and hauled myself woozily out of bed
to face the blazing summer and set off for Blackrock with two
friends, Gerry and Gob.

Outside the slaughterhouse we were approached by a police
sergeant.

'Have any of ye seen a quare-looking lad, older than
yerselves, coming along this road a while back?'

We stood and thought, visibly. Guards were not men to
mess around with. We had seen no one on the way into
Blackrock but we were determined to fit someone into the
Guard's description. However, try as we did, we couldn't.

'No. We haven't seen anyone,' said Gerry.

'Nope. Sure haven't,' said Gob, Western style.

The Guard gave him a look as though marking him down
as a smart fella who would one day need a clout.

'What's up?' we all wanted to know.

The Guard dismounted from his bike and twirled the pedal
around to park it at the pavement. He surveyed us as if unsure
whether we were old enough to be involved in grown-up stuff.
He looped a finger into his breast pocket while he thought.

'Has there been a robbery, has there?' Gerry's excitement
let us down. The day promised to turn into something worth-
while but there was no need for Gerry to jump up and down
like a kid.

'Indeed there has not!' The Guard laughed, showing a gap
in his front teeth. His accent, like all Guards, was resonant
of country parts. We didn't dare even to think the word
'culchie', lest he should read our minds and and clove us in
two where we stood.

151

'No, no, no. No robbery. Nothing at all like that. No, it's just that a lad has run off from St John's up in Carysfort and they say he came down this way.' We exchanged looks. Gerry looked grim and serious. A loony was out. Right here in our own neighbourhood there was an escaped lunatic.

Mr O'Flynn approached us from the door of his bicycle shop across the road. He was as excited as we were.

'I hear one's slipped away on ye,' he said, treating the Guard with a familiarity that I felt marked him down as a spy and an informer.

'He hasn't slipped away on us! We don't look after them ye gobdaw! It's the Sisters you should be criticizing. It's their responsibility. We only clear up the mess.'

O'Flynn rubbed his hands and drew his breath over his teeth and shook his head.

'Ah, of course it is now. I was only getting a rise out of you. Of course it's the Sisters. A great and thankless job they do too. Jasus now if I had me way I'd ship the whole lot of those loonies off to one of the islands off Galway or somewhere like that. Dump the lot there and let them look after themselves. The government have no business putting them down among normal people. What are they thinking of at all? Who wants to live near a bunch of headers, eh?'

The Guard looked at us and then turned back to the ferrety figure of the bicycle repair man.

'What kind of talk is that for children? Listen now. Firstly the government didn't put them here and secondly you have a fine attitude towards my home that you think that you can go dumping who you like there, eh?'

Too late, O'Flynn realized his mistake. He turned to go but the Guard held his arm. We sensed the man's discomfort and sniggered and nudged one another. The Guard pulled his man to him.

'Have some pity man!' he roared. 'Have some sense of Christian feeling. The poor lad we're looking for out there is just a little bit touched in the head. Half turned in the pan. Do ye follow? There but for the grace of God. Do you get my meaning. Sure who's to say that we're not all a bit soft, eh?'

'Oh, you're right there and no mistake,' O'Flynn squirmed in the vice-like grip round his elbow, 'you're exactly right. It could happen to any of us.' Abruptly the Guard released him and the bicycle man staggered slightly. The Guard grinned down at him.

'Good. I'm glad you agree with me so.' He winked at us. We laughed, happy to be sharing the joke. O'Flynn darted a look up and down the road and then shot back across to his shop. The Guard watched him go. 'Bloody eejit,' I heard him mutter. Then he seemed to remember. He drew himself up and looked serious.

'Anyway, boys, there's a fella out from the home so spread the word and be sure to let the Guards know if you see anything. Don't go chasing him now.'

We stayed very close together as we turned back for home. Dark clouds rolled in from nowhere over us and the fun went out of the day. It was all we could do not to run while the Guard was still in sight.

We passed a butcher's boy and I eyed him suspiciously until he spat in my direction. I avoided his eye in case there was a claim to be made. He cycled on without a backward glance. I imagined him spitting in people's meat.

It was one thing to have a mad relative in the family. Clare Sheehan might be a bit soft and sometimes a tiny bit creepy but we could never imagine her doing anything really bad. Lots of people had an aunt or a grandad who were a bit gone in the head. One stick short of a bundle. Real madmen. Lads from up in St John's were another matter.

You only had to look into those mad faces, with their strange, frightening grins to know that you could never trust them. The papers were full of horrible murders done by madmen. Were not these young lads the same? They hadn't done anything we knew, but they were capable of any abomination. Precisely because they were mad. The only reason they weren't in the papers was because they hadn't had the chance yet. When one escaped it was time to be on your guard.

The loonies lived behind high walls and were looked after by tired little Sisters and when they walked out on the streets they held hands like babies. Some of them dribbled and they groaned and moaned and shouted as they stumbled along for their airing by the sea. All of us lads knew that loonies smelt of shit because they were always doing it in their trousers.

When we got to the terrace there was such an air of expectancy that I half expected to see an invasion fleet moving in across the Bay. All the adults were out on the steps talking of nothing else. No one said anything to us and we slipped in around the crowd but were shushed away and took up positions on the lawn.

Liam and his friends were telling tales of famous madmen. One who'd gone berserk and slaughtered his entire family with a carving knife and had then sat down to read the paper. That had been in Howth.

Then there was the fella who'd broken into a graveyard to eat the bodies, and yet another one who had to be kept chained up in the smallest room in the Institution because he destroyed everything he touched.

There was a sudden explosion of hoots and shouts. Voices dropped lower and lower and then there'd be an almighty roar and they'd all jump as the teller reached the punch-line.

Across the road I felt the hair rise on my neck and cast furtive glances behind me. Gob and Gerry began to tickle and punch one another and creep up on me with their tongues slavering. Or they'd pretend to go mad themselves and put on mad, staring eyes and reach with grasping fingers for flesh. The adults thought this was hilarious and we were allowed to edge into their company.

Led by Liam and his friend, Jim, we all went out on to the road. They all hung about with their hands plunged into their long trousers. We clambered into a tree and hung, upside down, from the branches.

A man on a bicycle arrived. A stranger. He was beside himself with excitement.

'They've got him! They've got the bastard!'

He was surrounded by a crowd, demanding the details.

'Over in the park. See for yourselves. Some lads have got him surrounded. I'm off for a Guard. Gotta go, lads.'

154

There was a charge down the Avenue to the park. A small park, no more than a field really. We poured through a gap in the railings.

In the far corner of the field there was a semi-circle of men standing alertly as though taking part in a ball game. Beyond them we could just make out a figure.

The lunatic was in his early twenties. He was dressed in shapeless trousers and a white open-necked shirt. He stood, thigh-high, in nettles. He smiled a strange, shadow smile at the circle, as though he were seeing something quite different and pleasant.

The circle swelled with our arrival. The madman suddenly looked a bit startled to find himself being looked at by so many. He frowned. They'd been doing that since he was a baby. Looking and peering.

We were silent. No leader had emerged so we just stood.

'The Guards will be here soon,' Liam offered, 'we'd best just keep him here until then.'

Danny, a hard-faced young Ted, was not to be put off. He plunged into the nettles towards the madman.

'Come outta that will ya!' he shouted, at the same moment lunging towards the madman's arm. Everyone tensed. Now was the time. Fireworks for sure.

'Christ!' Danny screamed, 'the fucker's bit me!'

'Let me at the shite! There's a belt for you. Come on lads, don't let him get away with it. Grab a hold there, Christy, so I can get a dig in!'

We all felt the hate now. Beat the bejasus out of the mad slavering dangerous bastard. Smash his skull in, he's hardly human at all. Better off out of it in any case.

There was a kicking and a punching in the nettles. We saw a face, still grinning, fall away. One blow smashed into the young man's head and he gave a twitch and lay still. The men stood back from their work, breathing heavily.

Danny looked at the stick in his hand as though someone else had put it there. He flung it over his shoulder. The madman lay crumpled at their feet. Now he was just a young man. Not mad at all. His face was bloodied and his mouth was open. Blood ran from his ear down his neck and into the ground.

'Come on outta that!' said Danny kicking him. 'Come on now and stop yer codding.'

Christy dropped to his knees.

'Jasus. I think you've killed him,' he said quietly.

'I hope, for your sake son, that you haven't.' It was the Guard we'd spoken with earlier. He stood there holding his bike. Someone moved forward and took it for him. Slowly he removed his bicycle clips and put them in his pocket.

'Ah, for God's sake, officer,' Danny began, his face red and his eyes darting around for support.

'Ah, for God's sake,' the Guard mimicked, 'you were just restraining the dangerous murderer until I got here. That was it, I suppose?'

Danny made to say something. But the Guard moved towards him and he fell silent. The circle widened. People made space, others quietly left the field by jumping over the hedge. The Guard said nothing. His gaze fell on me for a second but he just shook his head. Then he knelt down beside the madman. Gently he stroked the hair from the man's bloodied face. He spoke without looking at us.

'Sure I suppose, as good citizens, ye were only helping the police. Is that what these good people were doing to you, son?' He spoke to the man on the ground now, no longer interested in us. His scorn withered us.

The madman moved. 'Jasus thank God!' O'Flynn piped up. I hadn't noticed him until now. 'I think the poor man's alive and I thought he was dead for sure.'

'Come on now, son. Sit up if you can,' said the Guard, lifting the wounded head up. 'Come on now and we'll take you home for a bit of a clean and some nice tea maybe. What about that?'

He helped the madman to his feet. He took his handkerchief from his pocket and wiped the bloodied features. The madman smiled at him but not at us. When he saw us he shied away.

'Now don't worry a bit. These nice people won't hurt you. They didn't mean it. Come on with me and we'll take you for a ride in a nice car. What about that, eh? It's not far, there's the good lad.'

The two of them walked to the bike and the Guard took the handlebars. He wheeled the bike and walked the madman towards the gate on the other side of the park.

A police car had arrived. Small and black. We watched while he handed his charge over to the other officers. He watched it go, then he turned and watched us.

Quietly the mob seeped from the park. Only when it was quite empty did the Guard mount his black bike and ride back up the Avenue to Blackrock.

31

'Grandma passed away during the night,' Mother said, plonking a brimming cup of mahogany tea beside my bed. Mother ensured that we rose every day by trawling the rooms at eight in the morning armed with a tray of tea. She preferred that we didn't appear in the kitchen. The feeding and watering of the aunt and two working sisters was too important.

The announcement of Grandma's death made little immediate impact. The old woman had never said very much since she'd come from the south. She was too old for me to know and although it was only four months since she'd come up, there was no surprise at her passing. She moved, silently, around the house in padded slippers whenever she was out of bed, which was rarely.

Usually we only noticed her at Sunday lunch. She would shuffle in to take her place at the end of the table nearest the garden door. A plate of roast pork would be set in front of her. All around her noisy children and grandchildren would fight and argue and bawl throughout the meal. She would chew away in a determined fashion until her plate was quite empty. She never lacked for a good country appetite. Then she'd sit back and fold her arms on her lap and listen.

Little was addressed to her directly but she would smile and nod away happily. Very occasionally, when the talk turned a shade rich for her sensitivities, a small vein on her forehead would throb disapprovingly and she would tut very quietly.

When she decided that she'd heard enough nonsense, and if the day was nice, then she'd take herself out into the garden and sit under a tree. There she would sit, as though sleeping, having a wonderful chat with her childhood friends.

'Will ye pop in and see her before you go off to school?'
Mother asked. I looked at my young brother. His round, red
face wore an angry and puzzled expression. Grandma's dying
was a baffling intrusion.

'Dead,' he said, as though he were trying to get hold of a
very slippery notion. 'Dead. Where? I mean how?'

Mother seemed happy to talk for a minute. Down below
we heard the rest of the family on the stairs and the bathroom
door opening and closing. Far away Liam lay snoring under
the weight of ten blankets, despite the heat.

'Oh, she's been very poorly for a long time now.' I couldn't
think of when this was, Grandma had always looked the same
little figure in her grey and navy.

'Doctor Fitzgerald says that she just faded away. The heart
was weak. I think it was the heart he said. But she'd been
very low for a while and I don't think those vitamin tablets
were right for her at all. They gave her stomach no peace
she said to me only last week.'

I could see her now. She had a frail, fine face with whispy
snow-white hair. She only wore glasses to read with and her
eyes were a deep blue. Now she was dead. Here with us in
the house. 'Will ye ever just pop in and say a Hail Mary?
Then I'll give ye a couple of shillings and you can go out for
the day with your pals.'

'But where is she? Where will we go?' My brother's voice
was nervous and unsure but there was still a hint of truculence
in it as though he still suspected a rather poor joke.

'Oh, she's below in the back bedroom as peaceful as can
be.'

As we dressed we wondered what she would look like. There
was a body here in the house. A dead human was below our
feet. There would be a funeral and everything. Would we
have to go?

'It doesn't matter to you, of course.' I said to him when we
were nearly ready.

'Why? Wotcha mean?' he spluttered.

'Well, you weren't related to her. Not really related. The
way I am and the rest of us.'

His face looked completely bemused.

'You were adopted and adopted people don't count.'

'Aw go and shite now! I'm getting sick of that one!'

Shouting and pushing and pulling we went downstairs. I pushed the door open very gently and smelt the air. I expected that there would be some recognizable smell of death, some sort of heavy odour to show that life was extinct here, but there was nothing. Just the usual room smell that all the rooms in our house had after forty years with the windows jammed shut.

We went in. The room was bright and sunny. I deliberately avoided looking at the single divan bed. I wanted to feel the room and to imprint this on my memory. There was a dead person in this room. A dead body. Somehow I felt that everything that had gone before was a build-up to this moment.

I turned and looked at the bed. Grandma was there all right. There was no question that she was dead. The two large pennies on her eyes were a giveaway. For one moment I thought that she was wearing some sort of sunglasses that I'd never seen before.

We both approached the bed. Her face was quite calm. Not the calm that is supposed to denote an inner peace. This was a calm neutrality, an indifference to the event.

We hovered by the bed, unsure of what to do. In films there was always a capable adult to direct operations but not here. Mother had gone about her business downstairs and left us to it. I wondered was there a book on how to treat dead people.

We knelt, self-consciously, by the bed and bowed our heads in silent prayer. I could think of no prayers at all. Instead my mind raced ahead to the funeral that was now going to take place. I saw a group in black, gathered by the grave with the wind howling and the rain pelting down. I saw a headstone on a bleak hillside. I was Alan Ladd in *Shane*, standing quietly in the background as sober citizens buried their own.

My brother was kneeling on the other side from me. I glanced across and caught him looking at me. It occurred to me that he expected some sort of lead. I coughed and nodded solemnly and then rose to my feet. Was she going to be left

160

here all day? There seemed to be a marked lack of urgency about the whole thing. I could imagine Mother leaving Grandma up here for several days. There didn't appear to be any of the people I associated with this sort of thing – doctors or priests – around. And where were the undertakers, for God's sake!

We both stood in silence looking down at the small country-woman who had come up from the south to die in our house. As I stood uncertain of what to do next I could hear, once again, that machine-like sound coming through the thickness of the walls from the Sheehans.

The moment was broken when Mother bawled up from beneath us that there was a fresh pot of tea brewed and some crusty white bread and marmalade. Relieved, we left Grandma lying in the back bedroom, and went off to slurp tea and pester Mother about what would happen to the body.

32

Grandma's funeral gave us the chance to ride in a Daimler. We all crowded in until the cool dark interior began to warm up quite quickly with the family's collective hot air. Father sat by the window and fiddled with his tie. He constantly pulled his beard away from the tight collar. Undaunted by the crush, Mother and the aunt sat squeezed together and smoked their way down to the church.

As we drove down to Blackrock people stopped to look at us. They blessed themselves and their faces were solemn. We were being noticed. I put on a serious face and nodded back at the passers-by. Once I raised a weak hand and feebly waved.

Outside the church two young men stood, oblivious to our tragedy, reading English newspapers full of smut and soccer.

'Street corner bowsies the pair of them!' Father snorted. 'No credit to their people I can tell you that.' He pursed his lips as he spoke. It gave him a slightly old-maidish look and his eyes gleamed a bit. He was the first to read those papers when Johnny Mac flung them on to the porch every Sunday. 'They're from across the square,' he said, clinching it.

Ah, Saint Anne's Square! An evil den of redbrick and green railinged legend. A gap in the main road that opened out into a triangle of council flats. Not a place for a nice boy to go nosing about, Father said. Not if he wanted to come away with his cobblers intact. Everyone knew that nice people had had to be rescued from in there, by the police no less, because there was nothing that those gurriers wouldn't get up to. They weren't afraid of the police. Not they. When they weren't hanging around smoking and shoving into people, they were, like as not, doing time in a reform school.

162

With a flare for the Victorian, Mother liked to call them 'industrial schools'. I imagined the grim outline of a Dartmoor fortress lost in the wildest part of Wicklow patrolled by Brothers with hurley sticks.

I was surprised by the crowd inside. I never dreamt that a Tuesday burial could find so many with so little to do. We walked in a very sedate column down the centre of the church watched by old, craning faces. Father and Mother led us down to the front. There, a plain coffin with brass plate and handles stood on a small trolley.

A Mass followed and as it progressed towards its finale the crowd quickly thinned out. They had only popped in from around about for the Mass. At the end, undertakers moved in and we followed the coffin back out into the cheerful sunshine. There the coffin was slid into the back of the hearse and a wreath placed on it.

The Sheehans approached and spoke to Mother. Her mouth set as she listened to them and her head tilted on one side as though she was having trouble following them. They were uncomfortable and made a hasty retreat when Father went over. There were other neighbours but few and they were there because they had business in the village. Only then did I really realize that my grandmother was not from there and no one had known her. I wondered if down in Kerry there was someone who might at that moment be lighting a candle.

We crushed back into the Daimler and followed the hearse slowly out the long road to the cemetery. This was the part that I feared. Sitting there I imagined dreadful scenes at the graveside but all around me the others chatted in quite a relaxed way. There was not even a suggestion of strain.

Mother said 'God rest her soul' once in passing but the rest of the journey was spent in small talk. Now, as we followed the hearse, people on the footpath took much more notice as though the coffin ahead confirmed our purpose. They stood and doffed their hats or blessed themselves. Oddly I enjoyed their respects as if they were meant for me. Inside, Liam pointed out a baffling array of buildings and landmarks as though he were on a coach tour with total strangers.

At the cemetery the weather continued to play havoc with my notions of tragedy. We stood around the grave squinting into the bright sun and listened to a short sermon from a rather bored young priest. No one seemed to notice his obvious desire to be elsewhere and before I was properly aware of it Grandma was lowered into the hole.

Father gave a rather theatrical trumpet into his handkerchief while Mother and Aunt stepped forward and looked into the hole as though to make absolutely sure that the deed had been done.

As we walked away all the adults lit cigarettes and inhaled deeply. Liam lit Mother's for her which seemed an oddly intimate thing to do, then offered his own pack around. Father took one and patted Liam on the shoulder. They walked ahead, heads bent, talking together, the loose ends of Liam's childhood falling away as they went.

'She was as well out of it,' Mother said.

'Ah, sure she'd lost interest,' said the Aunt. 'Dublin never really agreed with her. She never really settled. So it was probably for the best.'

'At least she didn't suffer and sure that's a blessing.'

'Oh, it is! It is! And not one to be taken for granted.'

The talk turned to acquaintances who'd had prolonged and agonizing pains before death had mercifully released them. I never realized how many of the neighbours had died so miserably.

They spoke of old folk who'd been left where they'd fallen until the smell had alerted neighbours. Men who'd cut their throats with huge open razors and then staggered out into the streets gushing fountains of blood on their neighbours. The ones who'd died of the fierce cold and turned blue. Then there was the not so old fellow who'd jumped under the Bray train and they'd been scraping bits of him off the line at Blackrock for weeks afterwards.

'And didn't old Mrs Taggart hang herself? I'm sure I heard that now.' There was nothing the aunt enjoyed better than a bit of death.

'Oh, she did. They cut off the pension she was getting since Charlie boy died and it was too much for her.'

'I thought that was the story all right.'

'She was a Protestant, you know,' said Mother.

'Oh, now I never knew that! You'd never have thought it to look at her. She didn't impress me that way at all!' My aunt was amazed at the news. Mother was pleased with her item.

'Oh, her people were, from way back. Of course, they've nothing to fall back on. That's the problem.'

'Who haven't?'

'Protestants. They haven't the Faith to see them through. They're too gloomy and wrapped up in themselves by half. That's the problem.'

'Aren't they plagued with it in England?'

'They're never done with it.'

33

So the long Dublin summer passed slowly, Liam picked up a rucksack after tea one evening, said goodbye, and caught the mailboat to England. His leather sandals slapped the garden path down to the back gate and then he was gone.

In the long pink evenings shoals of porpoises dived and cavorted in the Bay drawing an audience of a thousand aimless strollers. Ties disappeared and jackets were carried over the arm. Women left their stockings over the ends of their beds.

The roads out from the city were crowded with straining cyclists all hurrying to catch a swim before the tide went or it grew dark. Mr Keely's station was constantly busy with travellers so that he hardly had a moment to put his feet up. Instead he spent his life on the platform making sure they didn't trample over his flower beds in their rush to the sea.

Horsemen called Desmond and Hugh raced one another along the sands and drove their mounts into the sea to splash and dance in distant, echoing glee. Then they would whirl about and race back at full gallop to Dollymount.

Father continued to write. Not so much on the steps anymore because of the distractions. 'Can't get a damn thing done there. No sooner do I put pen to paper than some codology merchant appears with nothing to do only gab the day away.'

So he moved back indoors and only came out in the evening to sit on the step and watch the Bay. Sometimes he would sit with a bottle of stout and pour it very carefully into a long glass. Then he would sip it slowly and comment on the yacht race taking place out by Howth. 'The red fella has it,' he'd say and nod at a crimson sail bulging with speed.

'That Castro fella is a right one all right.' Mulcahy would remark.

'I suppose you think the Yanks will step in.' Mr Mac sneered. He had little time for Mulcahy or his views.

'Oh, Kennedy's the man for those boys. We could do with him here.' Mulcahy beamed, happy to be on both sides at once.

'There's nothing wrong here that couldn't be cured with a bit of sense,' Jack put in. He couldn't keep the irritation out of his voice. 'We don't need a Yank to bail us out every time something goes wrong.'

'But isn't he one of our own?' Mulcahy offered.

'Which means exactly nothing! Oh a very great honour for Ireland no doubt but don't expect him to take any interest here. He'll have his hands full enough as it is. Trouble with this blasted place is we're always pining after leaders.'

'Oh you're in a mood today, Jack, you don't want to take politics seriously at all,' Mr Mac grinned at him.

'Well it makes me spit. They were in such an all-fired hurry to shunt the Boss out of it that they forgot that they might have to put something in his place. So the best they can come up with is the great Economic Plan. Plan my eye! They couldn't find their arses with a map!'

The other two laughed at this. He felt annoyed that he had to put things in such a cheap way to get a laugh. On the other hand if he didn't they would think him distant and he didn't want that. He wanted to be an ordinary chap who just happened to write.

He was amazed by the ignorance and simplicity of the views expressed and couldn't understand how they had come so far knowing so little. Mulcahy was a thick. Plain and simple. The man never opened his mouth except to deliver himself of some totally banal remark. Anything, other than a gut reaction to screaming headlines, was beyond him. Mac was one of those who especially irked him. Mac had a reputation as a sophisticated man with a taste for good suits and club life. His one aim in life was to give the impression that he knew much more about things than he let on. He would comment and then give a short, dry laugh and shake his head as if to indicate that he was keeping back the best because it was a secret.

Mac kept his affairs fairly murky but liked to describe himself as an all-purpose businessman. No one knew where he operated from or what line of business he was in but the man never seemed short of a bob or two. Whereas Mulcahy made a pittance on the council, Mac always had an ample supply of serious dough to flash about.

Mac was wearing brown suede shoes. Brown suede shoes with a tweed suit. That was typical of him. He was probably playing at being the country gent today. What the hell am I sitting here wasting time with these two gobshites? Mac was no more than a spectator of life. He had no real opinions on anything and never said anything until he was sure of the ground. His caution didn't sit well with the rakish air he liked to give off.

'Still and all it's a great thing for an Irishman to be the President of America,' Mulcahy chuntled on. 'A great thing and I don't care who knows it.'

'Oh, for God's sake, man, no one's denying that! Great. Brilliant. Fabulous altogether.' Mulcahy looked pleased.

'You agree with me then?'

He looked at the round face.

'Well now, that's grand then.'

'But Mulcahy.'

Mulcahy bunched his eyes and concentrated.

'Kennedy's about as Irish as the Duke of Wellington.'

Even Mac looked outraged at this. For a second he seemed on the verge of offering an opinion.

'Ah, would ye get away out of that,' Mulcahy's whole body leant away in disbelief. 'You're a terrible man for the strange and rare ideas Jack, I'll say that much for ye.' He laughed as he said it. Happy and simple.

'I mean what I say. John F. Kennedy is Irish in the same way that the Duke of Wellington was a Dubliner.'

'Ah, come on now, Jack. You're not talking sense.' Mac was speaking at last. 'Everyone knows his people are from Wexford.'

'His people are from Wexford,' Jack repeated in a scornful tone. He was aware of it. 'Are they now? And what the hell does that mean. I mean what the hell does having people from somewhere down in God-knows-where mean?'

'Sure that the man is Irish, Jack,' Mulcahy said anxiously.

'Look, lads, the Kennedys this fella came from are a Boston family who are millionaires. Multi-millionaires for all I know. They live in huge houses. Travel in the highest society. Own racehorses. The last one of them to have a trace of an Irish accent died over a hundred years ago for God's sake. The man would be as out of place here as you would be if I set you down in the Arabian Desert this instant. He couldn't give a tinker's about this place so don't expect him to rush over and offer us this, that and the other. Because he won't and who's to blame him?'

Mulcahy and Mac looked at one another uncomfortably.

'Don't you see it men. His family left because there was nothing here for them. He'll not come rushing back now righting wrongs. My point is that we've got to do it for ourselves. You can't throw out the Big Fella and then expect a lot of nonsensical plans dreamt up by college boys to work.'

'Ah, you might have a point all right and I'm not saying you don't but if you go down the country now you wouldn't find many people who'd agree with you, Jack.' The serious tone in Mulcahy's voice made him look up. He had offended his neighbour. Mulcahy liked things kept friendly. Mac sensed the mood and made to move off.

'Ah well, it's just an opinion, lads. Nothing more. Nothing more.'

'Well, I'm away home now all the same,' Mulcahy said, moving away.

'Me too. I've a game of bridge to get to.' Mac straightened his tie and said 'Good luck' over his shoulder as he trotted off around the corner. He could imagine Mac playing bridge and holding the cards in a fan below his shifty eyes.

He turned his attention back to the Bay. His son and a crowd of others had gathered on the bridge. There were adults there too and over on the railway bridge more people were looking down at something happening down on the rocks. He pulled himself up and went to see what the commotion was.

34

If Frank Chambers hadn't been so fond of making dramatic gestures we wouldn't be in this stupid position now, thought Jim Byrne as he helped to heave the canvas canoe into the water.

Everyone on the shore had seen the shark's fin cruising up and down the Bay all evening but only Frank had capered about waving his home-made harpoon and bewailing the lack of a boat. Naturally he'd attracted the attention of the other onlookers and in no time at all they'd been leant the canoe and urged to take action. The dare took on its own momentum. There was no question of backing out of it. Willing hands were holding the canoe steady for them to climb in. Opinions were divided.

'Killer whale, if you ask me. Probably drifted off course. Begod I wouldn't get in the same ocean as them, never mind the same Bay.'

'Getaway outta that,' said Jack Culhane, 'it's only a basking shark. Completely harmless.'

Jim was thankful for this comment but Jack went on. 'Mind you, you'd want to steer well clear of the skin on them. It would skin you to the bone if they so much as brushed against you.'

Great, thought Jim, there's always some snag.

Frank squared his shoulders and began to search the sea with a hand over his eyes. He nodded several times to himself. He felt the tip of his spear and nodded back to Jim. Jim began to row, wobbly at first, but with growing confidence.

As they pulled away from the shore Jim noticed that Frank had begun to somehow shrink in front of him so that now he sat hunched down in the boat with only his head, knees and the spear showing.

Frank was thinking to himself that he'd never really thought about just how deep the Bay was and that eighteen was really a bit on the young side to die. Jim wasn't even that. Not until sometime in November at any rate. Oh, to hell with Jim's birthday. He glanced around and saw Jim's sheet-white face and, over his head, the wobbly outline of the now distant coastline. How he ached for the shore as much as if he'd sailed around the globe.

He looked ahead. The fin was still there. That was almost a relief. Christ the trouser-browning thought of that giant fin lurking somewhere beneath him! Breathing and pulsing below. It was now only a couple of hundred yards ahead and to port. Frank could have sworn that it was much farther out. The rough and knobbly fin stood at least four feet out of the water.

Jim paddled on. Only last week he and Frank had sat in the balcony of the Pav and watched *The Creature from the Black Lagoon*. Oh, what a laugh it had been! How they'd rollicked in the aisles and thrown cartons at the screen when the creature lolloped along the bottom of the lagoon after its prey. Not so amusing now.

Pride drove them on. The shame and humiliation of it would be too much to bear if they had to turn back now. How could they face their admirers on shore if they paddled in with limp tales of how the great creature had disappeared under them and had swum out to sea. It would never be enough to claim that at least they had come this far. The Culhane girls had been watching and they wouldn't be taken in by such deceit.

Jim imagined binoculars trained on them right now, watching their every move. Their sweating, frightened faces were being scrutinized from the shore. Mr Roche had a pair and would be passing them around.

Jim's brain tried to think of jazz rhythms. He could see Fats Domino but even the great man's best tunes refused to form in his head. He could think of nothing except the shark. The back of Frank's head gave nothing away. He couldn't show himself up. He wouldn't be the one. He paddled on.

Each time he plunged the oar blade into the sea, he hoped it would break or crack or somehow weaken. There'd be no shame if they weren't able to paddle properly. The oar remained firm and solid.

He tried to crane over Frank's head but Frank was sitting up now and it was difficult. The thought of gaping jaws out there made him ill. He stopped paddling. Frank turned around and Jim saw the fin.

'I'm not sure about the point of this spear,' Frank said. Jim's chalky face and quivering lip offered the perfect out.

'Listen. Are you all right?'

Jim said nothing but continued to stare at the fin, which was moving away now.

'I was saying that the spear's banjaxed. What do you think? Jim? Jim!'

Jim looked at the spear tip. Frank pointed.

'See there. That's loose if you ask me. I wish I'd noticed that before we came all the way out here. Now the bloody thing'll get away.'

The crafty fox, thought Jim to himself, the sneaky fucker. He must have done that right there in the front. They were heroes again. They could step back from the brink. The spearhead was definitely loose. No use at all for the job.

'Damn,' he heard himself say, 'all this way for nothing.'

'Yeah,' said Frank, in disgust. 'I wish I'd checked the damn thing first.'

Jim knew his own way from here.

'Well, I suppose we could try and repair it but that would be pushing it. The bloody thing'll be gone by the time we get back.'

Frank scanned the sky and breathed in exasperation.

'No. More likely we'd be caught by the light and we'd not have a hope of tracking it in the dark.'

Jim considered this.

'Yer right there, sure enough, but what if I got that big torch of my old fella's. That's got a hell of a beam.'

Frank saw the bluff coming.

'Good idea. Except for one thing.'

Jim leaned forward, the better to hear the welcome snag.

'By the time we got back out here Moby Dick would be in Wales.'

They both sighed loudly as they realized that their prey was going to elude them. Jim spun the canoe about. Both remembered Roche's bins. Frank grasped the spear and shook it out to sea while Jim stood up in the canoe and waved in rage.

Frank had to grab the sides of the canoe to steady it and in doing so he let go of the spear which slipped over the side and sank, slowly. They saw the pale shaft vanish about six feet down.

The thought of what lay beneath them came back as they realized that what little armament they had was now gone. There wasn't another ship or yacht in sight. The fin seemed to be turning back towards them as if it knew. The Bay held only sunset, themselves and the shark. The breeze made them shiver.

Bollocks to Roche and his ruddy binoculars! There was nothing for it now. Jim began to paddle, fast. His arms flailed but the damn oar wouldn't bite into the water. He kept skimming with one side and dipping too deep with the other.

'Go on will you!' Frank urged, from behind.

'Will ye get knotted. I'm going aren't I?' How he wished there were two oars. He stopped for a moment.

'What are you doing?' Frank shrieked in his ear. There was real fear in his voice. Jim was angry.

'Well, if you're in such a bloody hurry, you can paddle your own damn boat!'

He didn't wait for an answer but passed the paddle backwards and let go. There was a muffled curse from Frank as he grabbed at it. The next instant they were underway again and Jim had to admire Frank's bullock-like strength for they fairly flew over the water. He could make out the shoreline now and as each piece became recognizably a part of another, his confidence soared.

'Oh the Yellow Rose of Texas, is the only one for me . . .'

He sang and beat time out on the canvas. He could feel Frank relax behind him as they approached the big rocks with their resident cormorants drip-drying their wings.

He wondered who would be on shore to greet them. The whole of south Dublin must have seen the shark. Maybe there'd be fellas down from the *Press* or *Herald* to interview them or take a photo.

Surely the Culhane girls might admire him now.

Kids swarmed around them as they landed and flung questions at them.

'Did ye hit it?'

'Was it huge?'

'Did it go for you?' they called.

At least it was a start and they both felt quietly pleased when the kids followed them up and over the bridge. Jim noticed the Culhane girls on the steps of their house. They were knitting. He and Frank both began to puff loudly, as though exhausted.

'Have fun, boys?' Anne asked, and then she whispered something to Mary and they both laughed. Jim felt his cheeks redden. He flung the oar away from him and left Frank to talk to the kids.

35

Father re-read the letter. The Principal Officer had noted his continued absence from his post and it was his duty, therefore, to request that he, James Culhane, should attend a medical tribunal on a date to be fixed. Otherwise, the letter went on, the Service would have no alternative but to dismiss him.

He put it down on the desk and stared at it. Blast! They were on to him. It was near enough a year since he'd walked out and he'd begun to harbour hopes that they would go on with the existing arrangement. Now they'd flushed him out. Probably some myopic little wages clerk with nothing better to do all day than to root out anomalies for his masters.

He knew something was afoot when his wife had handed him the envelope that morning. Her lips were pursed and she had a knowing, I-bet-this-is-serious-don't-say-I-didn't-warn-you look as she passed it to him. She had an instinct for disaster and it hadn't let her down. At least she had the grace not to hang around and make him read it to her. She wasn't that malicious and for that he was thankful.

The letter sat on top of his manuscript. For a moment he gave way and cursed and railed. Novel! What bloody novel? That was it. The small-minded, bitter, twisted pygmies had won the day. Another contribution to Western civilization shelved for want of a grain of understanding and support. By Jasus they'd regret this. He'd have a puss on him that would stop a dogfight for the rest of his life. They'd regret forcing him back.

The mood passed and depression drowned the anger. He couldn't see himself holding court to the literati of Dublin now. He would be a laughing stock amongst gobshites like the Sheehans. Oh what sport they would make of it when they found out. And they would find out. There was absolutely no doubt about that. The bandanaed loon was probably on the other side of the wall with a glass hoping to overhear something. As for Sheehan himself, he'd snort into his brown moustache when he sobered up long enough to hear the news. Culhane's had to go scurrying back to his work before they fire him out on his arse! He could hear the mocking voices now.

He strode to the wall and gave it a vigorous slap with the palm of his hand. There was an explosive crack. That'll give her something to listen to, the mad bitch! His hand felt numb with the shock and he sat down to rub it.

Then he heard the sound. The same sound that they'd all been hearing for several weeks now. What the hell were the Sheehans up to? By the sound of it they were operating a small steam engine. He imagined squads of sweating Sheehans feeding a blazing furnace in a desperate attempt to dry out their wet hulk of a house.

'Well?' his wife said from the doorway.

'Well what?!' He was irritated. He hated the way she seemed to materialize out of the carpet.

'You know perfectly well what. I'd be obliged if you'd keep the rest of us informed of our situation.' She took up station on the edge of a chair by the door.

He told her what the letter had said.

'It's just as well that your sister-in-law is working and that Liam can send the odd couple of pounds from London. If it wasn't for that we'd all be reduced to tinkers like the Falveys with not enough string for a belt.'

There was nothing he could say. She was absolutely right and he knew it. He shrugged and sighed heavily. She had, after all, managed to hold everything together with her mad system of cigarette-pack accounting and her absolute confidence that shopkeepers existed solely to serve her.

'The girls will be gone soon, so that's another expense less to worry about.'

He nodded along, hoping to deflect her anger by taking an interest. She was being reasonable. So much so that he felt a great surge of affection for her and he enjoyed the feeling.

'You'll have to get straight in and see the Principal or whatever he is and square things with him. There's a train into town in twenty minutes. Sure you could be in in no time.'

Her voice was both brisk and encouraging.

So that was it! He was being turned out. Sent back into that wretched office to face the scorn of the others. He squirmed, unable to match his rage with words, unwilling to start an open row. Her eyes were fixed on him waiting for an answer. He wished he could go out and come back in to start this whole conversation again.

'Ah sure I can't go back in at this time of the year. There's all, all . . .' he searched for some mysterious office process that she wouldn't understand, 'all the quarterly assessments going on.'

'The what?'

'The quarterly assessments. The time when they go through all the inter-Departmental Internal Evaluations.' That should do it.

She folded her arms.

'Jack, I haven't a clue what you're talking about but what I do know is that sounds like a load of ruddy nonsense. I've never heard such a ridiculous excuse. Sure what's to stop you going in no matter what time of the year it is? Jack, we need your salary you great, stupid man! We need it badly. I can't go on running this place on a shoestring and handouts. Don't you understand? It's over. Over and finished.'

'What is?'

'Try not to act completely thick, Jack.'

'I'm not with you. Really, I'm not.' He felt his heart racing.

'All this.' She waved at his manuscript.

'It takes time. I just need one publisher.'

'Oh, for God's sake, man! You've had time and buckets of it. Look, you come marching in here one dark evening and announce that you're not going back to work. You're going to stay at home and write you say. There's more to life than office drudgery. Fine. Well, let me tell you, there's plenty who'd jump at office drudgery and be glad of it!'

'But you know these things don't happen overnight.'

'But you've not done anything. You've fiddled around up here day after day and when you're not here you're down in the library or more likely the pub. I don't have to be a writer to know that it takes hard work. Bloody hard work, not roaming around Blackrock or drawing little pictures!'

'How can you say that? How can you say that? Oh, I knew you were against what I was trying to do all right but I thought that once I'd started you'd make some effort to support me. Instead of which I've had nothing but the Siege of Mafeking all bloody year!'

'That's so typical. Rant and rave. Forget the truth. What the hell does that matter when we can sit here and listen to your version. Did it never cross your mind to discuss your great plan with me first? No, of course it didn't. That would be too much like common sense and decency.'

'Ah it just boiled up inside of me. I couldn't take any more of that place. I just had to get out. I know, I should have discussed it with you.'

'You don't know what it's like going into the shops around here and having everyone asking how's Jack getting on with the writing. Do you know they hardly bother to hide the great amusement they get out of it? I can't go to Mass without being quizzed by a half a dozen people. I'm tired of it, Jack. Sick and tired. It has to stop. That's all.'

She lit a cigarette, shakily, and waited.

He couldn't think of anything to say. He felt cornered. Out of the window a flotilla of yachts raced across the Bay. A wooden car bounced along the drive. Children played outside on the lawns. Jim Byrne was trying to chat up the girls again. He could hear his young crow of a son shrieking from the highest branches of the big elm.

'Oh, for God's sake, don't just sit there! You must have something to say.' She pleaded with him.

He adopted a hangdog expression, hoping to deflect her.

'It could be worse, you know.' There was warmth in her voice now and he felt himself respond to it.

'After all, it was a good position. We all have to work for a living, I'm afraid that's just a fact of life.'

'It shouldn't have to be.' He knew he sounded silly, childish.

'Well, there's nothing you or I can do about that. Now is there?'

'No. I don't suppose there is.'

'If you really want to write sure there's nothing to stop you now.'

'How do you mean?'

'At the weekends. Liam is gone now and the girls will be in Paris very soon. We can set this room aside with everything you need. You could get a pile of work done at the weekend if you put your mind to it. And then, perhaps, when you do get a publisher interested, then you can review the whole situation again.'

He was doubtful, though he knew everything she said made sense. She extinguished her cigarette and rooted in her purse. She passed him two pounds.

'Now. There. Go on down to Blackrock and have yourself some pints and have a good think about it.'

'What about the summer holiday?'

'Well, there's not much in the way of money, you know.'

'I know that. But I could borrow a car and we could all go down to Cork.'

'We'll see how it goes. Go on before I demand a refund.'

As he rose to go she was smiling. With him, at him, he didn't know but he hadn't seen her smiling for a long time and he kissed her cheek as he passed to the door.

36

In the Sheehan house the boiler had never recovered from the beating it had taken when the roof caved in with the thaw. Sheehan had erected an elaborate construction of planks and poles, propping and bracing it. Ropes were attached to nails hammered into walls and then wrapped around the tank itself.

In an effort to dry out the house Mrs Sheehan kept the boiler as hot as she could. Prowling the ruined upper floor of the house she hoped one day to re-occupy it. She often sat amid the timbers and rubbish for hours at a time and her singing would attract Clare who would come and lie with her head on her mother's knee.

Mrs Sheehan took a curious comfort in Clare's indifference to her surroundings. Her daughter had been afflicted cruelly enough by life and it seemed to Mrs Sheehan that if this latest catastrophe didn't affect the poor girl then she herself wouldn't let it get her down.

When she had finished humming a Puccini aria she stroked Clare's hair for a while. Then she rose and felt the walls. The boiler didn't seem to be making much of a difference. They still streamed with damp. Pigeons still nested above her.

She looked up at the open sky above her. When she had been a girl her parents had taken her to the opera. They had holidayed in London before the war. Her father had been given tickets. She thought that made him a very important person. They had gone to Covent Garden.

It had been like every fairyland that she had ever imagined. Her father had worn evening clothes and her mother a long silk dress. It had been *Cosi Fan Tutti*. She'd loved it: the men in their silk knee breeches and the women with their hair piled high on their heads shaking their fans.

In the background there had been a scene with a blue sky. Looking up from the darkened room, through the gap in the roof, reminded her of that contrast between light and dark she'd felt in the theatre that night.

Up above her small, whispy clouds scudded past. Headed out across the sea to England. By nightfall they might be great banks of cumulus over the River Thames. She sighed.

'Nice,' Clare was beside her. 'Nice, Mummy. Clouds.'

'Yes, lovely clouds.'

Clare could be such a child sometimes that she shuddered to think what might happen to her. But she shrugged it off when Clare bustled out of the room and went downstairs. Things were all right again. The girl would get by, even if she was a bit slow.

The noise really was getting a bit much. The boiler was crashing away and making the most frightful racket. She'd already been glared at across the yard by the Culhane woman. Mind you, she was always glaring.

Mrs Sheehan descended the stairs to the drawing room to talk to her husband about it. Above her the boiler began to rock and vibrate. Ropes worked loose from nails. Other nails were wrenched out of wood. Planks cracked and supporting poles slipped, then fell.

Manufactured to the highest standards by Evans and Thompson of Bolton, the boiler was not meant to be subjected to such treatment as it had lately received in the Sheehan house. An industrial revolution had been needed to make it. Shepherds had been thrown off their grazing land to make way for the first Evans factory. If a boiler had been capable of thought then it would have thought that the Sheehans were no respecters of pedigree.

Downstairs Mr Sheehan lowered himself into an armchair with the *Irish Press*. He topped up his gin with just a touch more tonic. The door opened and his wife appeared.

Feeling very jovial, he said, 'Gone for the orange bandana today, eh? Very fetching. Really very chic.'

His wife ignored him. He never heard what she said or

181

what she was going to say because at precisely that moment the Evans and Thompson boiler, having ensured that everyone was safely downstairs, gave up the struggle and exploded with a shattering crash that ripped open the metal and sent the tank hurtling from its mountings. It rose briefly then came down, demolishing the bannisters in its path. Hitting the landing below, it bounced once and sailed through the front window where it landed on the drive below with a heart-stopping metallic crunch.

The TEK dairyman's horse promptly reared up and sent the contents of the float on to the drive where hundreds of gallons of foaming milk and shattered glass surged forward to engulf the ripped boiler in a white tide.

For a moment there was silence, then the terrace filled with neighbours. From every window there poked a head and at every door there appeared people. From each end of the terrace they approached the carnage. They circled it cagily afraid that there might be another explosion. Accompanied by warnings from the others, Mr O'Toole, who had retired from the railways and might be expected to know about boilers, went up to the wreckage and pronounced the danger over. Then everyone else came up and stared down at the steaming jagged metal and the bubbling milk.

Mr Sheehan appeared on the step of his house. He still held his gin in one hand and his paper in the other. His mouth hung open and he tried to say something. His legs wobbled and he sat down, heavily, on the step.

The spell was broken and people rushed forward to help, glad to be able to do something. As they did so Mrs Sheehan appeared, floating out from the clouds of steam in her hallway. Her orange bandana intact, she emerged serenely and calmly took in the scene. Then she patted her husband on the shoulder muttering 'There, there' and walked very sedately across the bridge to look at the sea.

Mrs Mac found Clare in the Sheehan back garden busily hoeing weeds in the borders and quite unaware of anything having taken place. In the days that followed the Sheehans were slowly helped to clear up and then to find somewhere temporary to live.

Mother even had the whole tribe in for tea while council workmen and firemen went through their house and surveyed the damage. The Sheehans sat in our front room and drank tea and ate mother's pink fairy cakes. Mrs Sheehan talked of the opera and ran on happily about returning to London for the season.

'I think she's cuckoo,' remarked the Aunt, as she made a fresh pot of tea in the kitchen, 'but then I always have.'

I looked into the front room. Mother and Father sat trying to make small talk with our neighbours. Mr Sheehan flinched when Father spoke to him, fearful of another punch. When none came he mumbled a reply and then sat ignoring everyone and staring into the fire which Mother had set, despite the sunny weather.

'Sure they've had no heat in that tomb of a place since the war I shouldn't wonder. Not the way he skimps on the rations.'

It didn't seem to me, lying on the floor, that there was any bad blood between the two families. They spent most of the afternoon chatting happily enough while pots of tea and dishes of cakes were ferried in frequently. As the afternoon wore on, even Mr Sheehan managed a thin smile once or twice.

Finally they rose to go. Clare knocked over her cup and there was a great commotion to make little of it. May giggled and blushed, while James, thin-faced and furtive hung back in the hall fingering the doorhandle. Mother and the Aunt ushered them out with waves and good wishes and reminders that they must call back should they need anything.

'Well now, that wasn't so bad,' Mother said.

'Not so bad at all,' the Aunt agreed, 'not when you think how potty they can be and indeed have been before now.'

'Bloody smuggler,' Father grumped.

The Sheehans moved that same week. The house was unfit to live in and they had to seek sanctuary with a squad of relatives in north Dublin.

'I can't imagine being related to that crew,' said Mother.

'How quiet they kept it. I never heard them mention any relatives. Not in twenty-five years.' The Aunt was distressed at this gap in her filing.

'Oh, I'd say the quietness was on the other side. Who'd want that lot calling in out of the blue.'

Mother's brief flirtation with charity had ended. She had spent several days hovering by the kitchen window as though hoping to catch a glimpse of an orange bandana. She sighed wistfully when none appeared but she quickly recovered and aimed her attacks at the empty shell of her neighbour's house.

'I'm not going to stand here and watch as the damp and God knows what else from that dump destroys us. What about your aunt's health?' she said one day. 'She's up near the roof.'

'Never bothered you before,' laughed the Aunt, breezing by in search of an ashtray. Mother looked outraged at this cut.

'Well, that's simply not fair. I've given it plenty of thought down the years.'

'Down the years! Down the years!' the Aunt roared, laughing. 'That's priceless. Down the years! Oh, that's the best ever!'

'Oh hump it! Don't deflect me. The fact is that wreck is having an adverse effect on us. It could ruin the value of this place.'

'Value! Mother dear, you've got to be kidding,' said Mary, whose suitcase upstairs was already half-packed for Paris. 'This isn't exactly the Ritz. Nor ever will be.'

'Oh, the sooner ye two are away out of it to Paris the better! You have me running backwards and forwards with your clever ways. Well, you'll soon see that it isn't as simple as that.'

Mother liked to finish on a mysterious note and she made to leave the room. Her exit was blocked by Father's bulk looming through her escape route.

'Holy mackerel! I've just noticed the date on this paper. We're over half way through bloody August! It's time for a holiday.'

He looked at Mother, waiting for a challenge.

None came.

37

The sun reflected a blinding silver on the dew-sodden lawns. At the end of the pier a body-laden mailboat slipped out of Dun Laoghaire on a flat, calm sea. A cargo of hope and necessity chugging gently over the horizon.

They would be late. Late. He'd said it of course but no-one had paid him a blind bit of attention and now they were running a real danger of having to stop over in some hotel or worse in Ballywhere'sthis.

It was going to be a hot day. Quite the best of the summer so far and that would be typical. Stuck in the car all day. He'd been careful with his dress but despite it his jacket already felt heavy and tight. He hauled himself into the driver's seat of the Morris and examined the dashboard yet again. It was a bit different from the Austin Seven. Quite different.

He fought down the rising panic he felt at the prospect of driving someone else's pride and joy to Cork. He fingered the gearstick and it felt all right. He pressed down the clutch and went through the gears. Then he peered at the ignition. Ah simple. Just make sure all the brakes were on and give the key a turn. He went over the procedures in his head then got out to help with the packing.

The children rushed out of the house and ran to the edge of the lawn. They scragged and wrestled one another. When he heard them talking about swimming out to the big rocks he ordered them, huffily, into the car. He instantly relented and let them sit in the front seat. Ellen had already taken up residence in the back with her sister. They were smoking and reading the papers and taking little interest in the proceedings.

Never mind me. I'll just do everything shall I, he huffed to himself. There was no point really. Details weren't the point on this trip, he thought, sweat bursting on his forehead as he squeezed the last of the bags into the boot. Details were not central. Not central at all.

There were much more important things waiting to be felt and experienced by an artist like him. He had to get out and touch his roots. They wouldn't understand, of course. How he had to feel, actually feel and touch old places and things to get the juices flowing. The city was throttling him that summer.

Anne and Mary were on the steps to say goodbye. They kissed him on the cheek, glancingly, and then leant in the back window to chat to the ladies. Everything would be fine, they assured them. They knew where everything was. After all, they would be in Paris soon. People in Monkstown did this all the time. Every summer and they heavily emphasized, 'every' for his benefit.

They stood back from the car, anxious for them to be gone. He climbed in and turned the key. It surprised, then pleased him to hear the engine come to life. He would have yelled in triumph but after all, it wasn't that different from a Seven.

The car felt good. Healy was a sound man. He hadn't hesitated for a second when he'd asked for the loan of the car. Healy had driven it out to the house a few evenings before. He wanted to stretch his legs so together they had walked along the seafront to Dun Laoghaire.

The Avenue had been thronged with white-shirted men and women in light frocks. They stepped into Smythe's and there they drank dark pints and talked. Healy was bursting to ask all about what he had been doing since he had jacked in work. He perched on his stool eager and waiting.

For a moment he was unsure of what to say but then his brain went for a walk. Paradise, he'd said. Paradise. If I'd known it was going to be like this I would have done it years ago. Every man should have a go at it and send the women out for a change.

They'd chuckled when he'd said that but as he sniggered he saw Ellen's face. His grin slipped. Healy had sensed that

186

something was not quite as clear cut as he'd been making out. He'd raised that damn rubber eyebrow of his.

Jack had looked away and cursed the Mayoman's speedy intuition. He wouldn't be able to resist spreading it around the office, damn him. Jack gulped his drink to gain a second or two. When he looked up the little countryman was still there, waiting.

'No, no! It's great. Really.' He'd tried to laugh it off. 'The writing is coming along brilliantly. It's great to have a bit of time and space to think things through and not be always worried about some damn manifest of goods.'

Healy brushed aside his enquiries about the office and by his silence forced him to continue.

'Yeah, a few publishers are interested in what I'm about. Nothing definite but you know what they're like!'

'That's great, so,' Healy had said, taking a great swig from his pint and standing it on the polished bar, half empty. Great, Jack had heard himself say again but with little conviction and the Mayoman avoided his eye.

He did manage to force the conversation around to the office but Healy would say little. They had discussed the car and what little quirks to watch out for.

'You'll need to pump the brakes because they're not what they were. But don't worry on that score, she's a great goer. Great altogether when you get on to a bit of open road.'

As he had listened to the car's foibles being outlined he had resented Healy. Quite unfairly, of course. The man was making the holiday possible after all. He didn't resent that. No he was grateful, naturally. It was just that he felt that Healy could see clean through him. It was as though Healy knew all about his showdown with his wife and knew that there were no publishers or much money coming in either. Healy represented safeness. He was the office. Jack knew that wasn't fair but he couldn't control his frustration.

He saw Healy on a city bus and waved him off with the promise of postcards. His friend had stood on the platform rolling to the rhythms like a sailor. The Mayoman had tossed his head in salute but his eyes had seemed to say that he had seen through some piece of fakery. The battered green bus bounced out of sight.

He'd felt the keys in his pocket but the excitement of it was quickly washed away by an image of his former colleagues doubled up with mirth as Healy told them all about his evening by the sea with Culhane.

He put Healy out of his mind. The car felt good. Christ, it must be twenty years since I did any real driving. This was good. Bit like a bicycle. There were dials and things he didn't recognize but the basic business was the same.

The kids sat up beside him chattering, their faces glued to the passing suburbs. He leant across and flicked open the glove box. Inside he'd placed a fat black leather notebook and several pens and pencils in an elastic band. That would keep him busy. He would drown himself in memories and allow the smell and touch of the old place to wash him clean. He hoped that somehow he would find the spark that was missing. He laughed to himself for not thinking of it before now.

'What's up?' Mother said from the back.

'Ah, nothing. Nothing at all,' he replied.

She didn't pursue it and went back to her newspaper. Occasionally she swopped remarks with the aunt.

They left the city. It faded away behind them in a line of crumbling stone walls and morose donkeys, grazing on waste land. The children's voices gradually faded away as the delights of their travel comics superseded the sights outside. He was left to himself in the front seat.

The road was empty and the car purred along. Healy certainly looked after it, he'd have to give him that. At Port Laoise he turned south for Cashel and passed its great rock just after they'd broken for a late lunch.

The children had begun to whine so they'd all piled into a run-down hotel where a snooty waitress let them know that they were lucky to get lunch at that hour because normally they stopped serving at two and she wasn't sure if the cook was still in the kitchen.

The meal was good but slow in coming. Perhaps they were being punished for their lateness, he thought. He had plenty of time to study the other faces in the restaurant.

Two old man sat together without a word and stretched their brace of pints through the Holy hour. He noted the different ways they drank, the one sipping delicately, the other with well-measured swigs. He wished he'd brought his notebook. This was just the kind of thing he should have been writing down. At least observing was a pleasure. He would get the details down on paper later. He decided they could easily have passed for a pair of clan elders discussing great hunting deeds of their youth.

Lunch finished, they pushed on farther and farther south, out of the lushness of the Golden Vale into a country of narrow high-hedged roads and stone walls. By early evening they were leaving Cork city behind and were hugging the banks of the Lee.

He found it difficult to drive when the sun was low in the sky. The road seemed to twist the car back into the glare no matter which direction they were going. He squinted out through the windscreen and leant forward in his seat so that his eyes were level with the top of the steering wheel.

'Mind out!' Mother screamed. He'd seen them and slammed down on the brakes. He felt the back of the car drift and then hold. He shot a hand across the kids and managed to stop them hitting the dashboard.

The gaudy caravans splurged on to the road in front of him, each wagon trailing bright colours and jangling pots. From each window, faces dark and smoky stared down at them. The children laughed and shouted.

'Janey mae! Look at them.'

'Just like in the *Hotspur*. They were excited. Here was something interesting to look at.

'My word but they're real gypsies now,' the aunt exclaimed.

'They nearly had us in the ditch! It's a good job the brakes work. The cheek of them! And no apology!' Mother said angrily.

The caravans moved slowly past them. He glanced up at a pair of eyes. Like black pools, dark and magnetic. He shivered. He'd never liked them much. They reminded him of something primitive, lost to the country now.

He thought of a Laurel and Hardy film where they'd been in a caravan filling wine jugs. The inside of the caravan had been pretty. A Hollywood set with a dresser of Delft. He didn't think these would be like that. These would be dark and fetid.

A dark man, like a Spaniard, in leather trousers, leaned out of the driving seat and spat into the hedge.

'Well,' said the Aunt. 'Really!'

They drove on. This time he went slower in case their path was crossed again by strange traffic. They were nearly there now.

Real gypsies. He wondered where they were headed. Even as a child he'd only ever seen tinkers, with their open carts and piles of scrap, on the roads. He didn't think there were any real gypsies in Ireland. What strange route had they taken from Hungary to end up in Cork? He wondered if they were a good omen, something exotic and outside the ordinary. The very opposite of the office. No, I mustn't, he thought. Such fanciful notions led nowhere and would only distract him.

At half past eight they pulled up in front of Feore's cottage. They stumbled in, numb with stiffness. He collapsed into a chair and allowed order to be imposed around him. A fire was lit and he was grateful for its warmth. In deference to his driving, tea and a sandwich were brought to him and later a bottle of stout. Gazing into the peat fire and sipping his bottle he felt peace and contentment for the first time in months.

For Father the holidays passed in a desperate pursuit of something that he could never recapture, the essence of his own childhood. He tried to keep his feelings to himself and made great fun out of the daily excursions around Charlestown and into Kerry.

Mother and her sister were perfectly happy to sit with relatives and drink pot after pot of tea. Father would stand at the window twisting his fingers behind his back and peering out, up and down the road.

They were lucky that the Feores still let out the cottage at a peppercorn rent. Jim Feore could have got much more for it and with each passing year the temptation for him to let it to tourists must have been getting stronger. But Jim Feore was a solid rock in a changing world. He had known him for years. That was one thing in the district that hadn't changed. They had shot rabbits together and those early, misty mornings were their bond.

The weather had turned mean and sour within days of their arrival. Great masses of dark cloud swirled in from the Atlantic patterned like glowering faces. He would look up at them and shiver before setting off on each day's mad drive through the lanes of the countryside.

As the others talked, smoked and played he sank into himself in the driving seat. He felt depression take him by the throat and squeeze. Joy and good humour seeped away and there was nothing he could do about it. He had to save the little left for when they were out of the car.

The holiday passed and as it did the desperation grew worse. He wasn't even sure himself what it was that he was seeking. He only knew that there must be something here. Something vital and real to take back to Dublin with him. He had not even opened his notebook.

He rushed about the countryside without any real plan, dragging his family with him. In every turning he searched for signs of his childhood and everywhere he went he was met by crumbling walls and strange faces.

He lagged behind at stops when the others moved off to explore. He knew he wasn't being much company but he was past caring. He was continually stopped in his tracks by small and insignificant things which left him standing in lanes shaking his head.

A signpost, fallen among bramble, would conjure up memories of a dance held in a hall long ago. A narrow track revealed a gang of happy youths walking abreast, carrying their shotguns. Bloodied rabbits swung at their belts. Jim Feore was the one laughing through his great horse teeth. Fred Callaghan was dead.

Two evenings before they were due to return he drove alone to the crossroads where his parents had had their house. He had deliberately left this until last. It was his house, he supposed though he had not lived there since his twenties. Then it had been in a poor enough state.

He pulled up across the road. The sun had made a determined effort and now shone bright and low in the evening sky. Its light edged the massed cloud with yellow and gold and reflected a pinkness in the stone of the house.

How low it was, he thought. The roof was in a terrible state, he noticed, crossing over. He stood outside and enjoyed the cool of the evening. There was a smell of burning leaves, sweet and sharp. God! Could it be autumn already. His heart leapt in alarm.

Crows and rooks gathered in great raucous black gangs that shook the trees they roosted in. There wasn't a soul in the darkening lane where the sun now slanted blindingly over the top of the hazel hedge and made him hold his hand to shade his eye.

He turned and looked away. There had been four families on this part of the Mallow road. All gone now. Two of the houses still stood but so altered by pebbledashing and slate roofs that he hardly recognized them. Of the other two, only the outline of one, covered in thick, green moss, now remained.

He went up to the door of his house. From the pocket of his thick jacket he produced the key. Still fits, still works. The door opened stiffly at first, then it swung inward.

The fireplace caught his attention first. It always had. A fire had been kept lit there permanently. Chopping logs had been a daily business. The grate was full of dust and soot but the flags on the floor were still smooth.

Cautiously he mounted the stairs. Two treads were broken. The landing at the top groaned under his weight. He pushed open his bedroom door. The tiny room was empty except for a tea chest which contained a blanket. He wondered how they had got there.

He had lain in here reading *Dracula* by candlelight fifty years before and listening to the howling storm outside. Later it had been Dickens. His father had bought the collected works for ten shillings from a travelling salesman.

He went to his parents' room. There was a huge hole in the floor, matched by one in the ceiling. The house was a wreck but even in that state he could still smell childhood.

192

This was what he'd wanted! He wondered why he'd left it so late. He went downstairs again and stood on the flags.

He closed his eyes and saw his mother marching down the lane in her heavy shoes and dragging him back to the house and away from his friends. She picked his company.

His splendidly uniformed father used to sit by the window at about this time of evening and smoke a pipe. An outline against a window. Always in the background of his life. A figure who sat in the kitchen and twirled his immense moustaches or who would spend hours cleaning his carbine and sprucing his kit. Then he would rise and go out to uphold the King's law. His mother was the law at home.

'Peelerboy! Peelerboy!' the kids had shouted at him even after his father had left the force to run a country store. There was revolution in the air and their elders put them up to it. Jack had ignored them. Ignorant farm boys the lot of them. He was going to the Christian Brothers in Cork city. They would spend their days with their noses to a plough. He had no need of them.

That was then. Now he wished he hadn't been such a little snob. The reality was that Jim and Fred had taken him shooting almost as a favour. The Woodbines he stole from the shop sealed the bargain and they accepted him. He'd known no other children in an area that swarmed with them.

It was nearly dark. He closed and locked the door behind him. He knew he would never come there again. The key was in his hand and he decided to give it to Jim Feore. He would be the best man to decide what to do with the place. Maybe the young lads in the district might have some use for it.

He got in the car and drove to the cottage. He didn't look back. As he drove he wiped a tear from his cheek and laughed.

38

On a moonless September night the desperate guardians of the National Will blew a wooden customs post to tiny pieces of matchstick all the while swearing vengeance for Sean South, their dead boy hero.

'Bloody Blackguards!' Jack swore as he read the *Independent* at the breakfast table. 'It's high past time that someone told those boys that all that stuff is as dead as the proverbial dodo. They're bloody hooligans bringing nothing but disgrace to us all. By God, the Big Fella wouldn't have stood for their nonsense.'

'How so?' Mother replied, feeling that someone had to say something. 'Sure it's been going on for years and no one seems to be able to do anything about it.'

'Indeed there's always hotheads ready to charge over the border fit for anything,' the Aunt added, dabbing her face with rouge.

'Your man up in the Park had the answer to those boys during the war didn't he? Up against the wall and a firing squad for them. He didn't pussyfoot around like this Lemass. *Gerrrrreerrrr!*'

Here Father made a sound like machine guns and shaping his arms like a rifle he moved his imaginary weapon in a slow arc while sighting down his sleeve.

If he had been honest with himself Jack would have admitted that he really didn't give a tinker's curse what the IRA did up there. He'd never really liked northerners as a breed. Humourless and hard he felt, they were welcome to each other.

'I thought I'd put the new sofa in the front room,' said Mother.

'What sofa? What do you mean in the front room?' He meant to say more. So this was it then. No drama. Just a sofa.

'I bought it at the auction last week along with a piano and they'll deliver it today sometime. Don't worry. There'll be plenty of room for your stuff. We can move you next door.'

'Oh, that'll be lovely,' Aunt said. 'Oh, my word! There's my train, I must fly!' She scooped her bag up and made for the hall. The train could be heard grinding in from Monkstown.

The holidays were long over. Mid-September had crept up on him. He knew he should be on the train. Mother continued brightly.

'Oh, I'm fed up with that other room. There's no comfort there at all. We'll do up that front room. The sofa will go nicely with the two armchairs and that means we can get us all in there instead of the squash we used to have. We can all be comfortable with the girls gone. And maybe I can play a little.'

The girls had crossed to France soon after the country holiday. Their delight at the prospect had been tempered a little towards the end when faced with the reality. For a moment he thought Anne might cry but she had recovered herself. They had both gone out to the taxi pooh-poohing warnings and admonitions. Their bags were full of guide books, maps and fashion magazines and each purse held several hundred francs.

Liam returned flush with money from England, smoking Gitanes. For several days he took his ease about the house. He read the *Telegraph* and tuned into the Home Service. Whitehall, Downing Street, Buckingham Palace and Harrods were all just around the corner from where he worked and lived.

'Did you get your ticket?' Mother asked Liam. 'I did indeed,' he replied, 'I shall be sailing at eight fifty-five tomorrow and thence to Euston.'

'Oh, that's quick,' Mother said.

'Yes. No point in hanging around. England, Father,' he added, seeing Jack's bewilderment. 'I'm going back to England.'

'So soon?' Jack was disappointed. The boy had obviously kept his plans from him. Dammit, it was clear everyone else knew. He tried to look hurt but Liam just shrugged and went back to his breakfast. The children rose and left noisily, for school.

Jack went through to the front room. He felt aggrieved. A bloody sofa! Squeezed out by a damn sofa. And a piano for heavens sake! He crossed to his desk and began to tidy up his pens and manuscript. All decisiveness now, he put everything into a cardboard box. A weekend writer. Well, maybe. He would be better prepared next time. He placed the box carefully in a cupboard. The library books he stacked on the sideboard. Then he went out into the hall.

She was at the kitchen door, watching him. He put on his overcoat and his hat. She said nothing. He said, 'See you this evening' and she smiled. Then he went to the front door.

Mr Keely said nothing when Father bought his ticket and boarded the 9.05 train for town. On the platform he held the door for him.